Wisconsin Iron

A Story of the Civil War

By

Michael Eckers

International Standard Book Number: 978-1453874738
Cover photo – Author's collection

To Diane

My wife of more than thirty years;
you remain the love of my life.

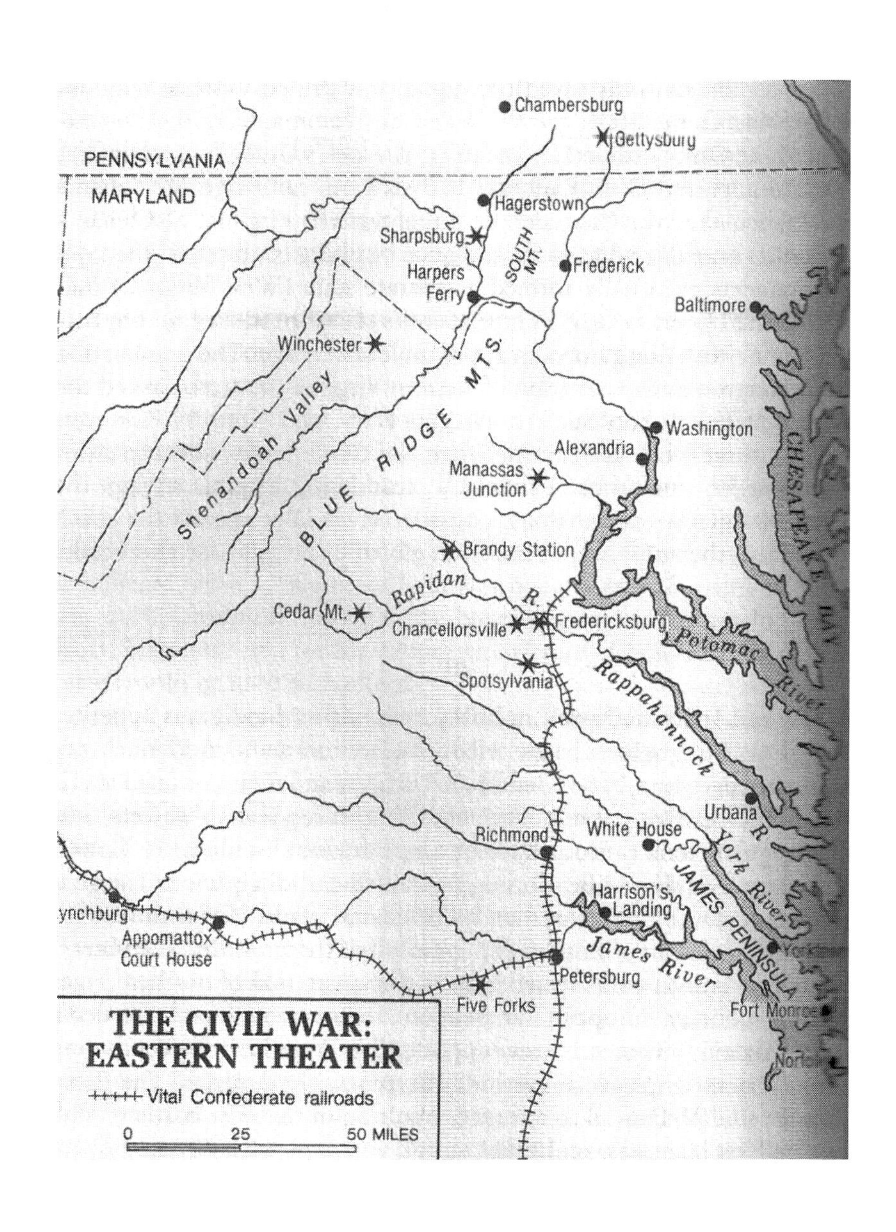

Map of the Eastern Theater

Introduction

July 1863

Henry ran for all he was worth. The bullets buzzed past and over him, chipping pieces of leaves and branches down on his shoulders and head. They sounded like a nest of mad hornets. He looked to his left just as a man who was only a few yards away threw up his arms and fell into a heap. The *regiment* had been ordered to fall back; they had pushed the *Rebs* hard through these same woods less than an hour ago. Now it was their turn to withdraw. Henry could see through the thinning trees ahead that the rest of the Second Wisconsin was reforming at the top of a small rise out of the woods; as a *skirmisher* he was one of the last to leave. He felt a bullet pass through his coat leaving behind a small burning feeling. Breathing was harder and his legs felt like they each weighed a hundred pounds. Now he was only a dozen or so yards from the others; he could see his uncle waving him on, encouraging him to hurry. Henry was sure the others were yelling for him as well but he heard only the sounds of the battle. He reached the line where they had reformed and turned to fire back at the approaching enemy. There were hundreds of them, in gray and butternut, just coming out of the woods. He could hear the *Rebel yell* as it poured out of them. Raising his musket he took careful aim, low, to be sure he hit his mark……

Chapter 1

April 1861

Marie McCullom wiped her hands on her apron as she went to the back door to call for her son. She had one fleeting thought of how different life was now; here she did the work with no help from servants. She so enjoyed the feelings of fulfillment the chores of love brought to her spirit. The sun was high in the clear blue sky and their noon meal of roast beef and fresh bread with jam was ready to eat. Her husband James was due home from his office next door any moment and it would not be pleasant if Henry were not here when he arrived. The boy, who just turned 16, was easily distracted by the river that flowed past the town of Dekorra. This time of year the fishing was particularly fine in Wisconsin and Henry felt there was nothing wrong with his attempts at providing food for the family; as though they wanted to eat fish every day. James had spoken a few days earlier that it was nearly time for Henry and himself to travel to Chicago to prepare for the boy's admission to Rush College to study medicine. James was a graduate of Rush, class of 1848, and had moved to central Wisconsin to begin his practice. One day his hope was to open an office in Madison, the state capital, which was about 40 miles straight south of Dekorra.

James came in the house and sat down at the table, mumbling a half-hearted greeting to his wife; the greeting of someone thinking of other things. She had not prepared an answer for the question of Henry's whereabouts she knew was coming. James didn't mention his missing son; he just sighed and rubbed his temples. "Difficult morning today?" she asked as he looked up to see her beginning to serve the meal.

"You've no idea. I was visited again by Archibald; he was on his way through here heading home to Poynette. He had just picked up his new *militia* uniform; it seems he's gone and joined the *company* of volunteers in Columbia County. He says there was news yesterday from Washington City that a fight could break out at any time down in Charleston harbor, you know, down in South Carolina. He feels a real shooting war is only weeks, maybe even days away. The militia is getting ready to move down to Madison if the Governor calls them to duty."

"Well, dearest, you know we've heard this talk before. The southern politicians always seem to call for a breakup of the *Union* whenever they want their way. Do you really think this time is different?"

Marie was genuinely interested in politics, something women were not regarded as knowing much about. She had been raised back east, in Boston, and her father had believed she needed a real education. When she and James first met, before he entered Rush College, there were moments when their talks veered away from love and future plans to discussions about the Missouri Compromise and Dred Scott. James grew to love his wife for much more than her beauty, which was breathtaking enough. Marie had been courted by several young men, most of whom were from "better" families than James'. Hers were the most incredible green eyes that contrasted and yet complimented her auburn hair. She was of medium height with a trim, almost delicate form. Marie would prove to have a physical strength to match her intellect. They had been married only a short time when they discovered the two of them would soon be three. Henry was born in the late winter of 1845, a few months after James began his studies at Rush.

Henry came through the kitchen door like a whirlwind, trying to catch his breath and talk at the same time. "It's unbelievable.....wonderful and terrible...never, ever....can't even believe it's happened....." He couldn't stay still, and kept hopping around and trying to talk but not having the wind for it.

"What in heaven's name are you going on about? You'd think the war has already started or something. Settle down and tell us what you've heard." James was just a bit annoyed, but the sight was too comical to be seriously angry with his son's tardiness for the meal.

"Just...wait....what..what war? Did the south start shooting? I haven't heard anything about that. Marcus and I were at the big pool and he just caught the largest pike we've ever seen!!! I can't believe they get that big." At that, all thoughts of his being late for the meal were forgotten; James and Marie could only laugh at the carefree life of their son.

When their meal was over James returned to his office to finish his day's work. Sometimes a "day's work" didn't end until well after dark. There had been several bad cases of measles over the past winter and James was the only doctor within miles. He was always welcome to stay overnight whenever the weather prevented his return home after caring for a patient; it was hard on him when ice storms and sickness combined to keep him from good rest. Thankfully, today was not one of those. He was looking forward to a relaxing evening; maybe he'd get Henry to show him where Marcus had caught that pike. It had certainly been a long winter with no fishing....

The door to his office opened and Archibald walked in. As tall and thin as he was, the nickname Arch was fitting; it seemed he was about to bend all the way over and form one you could almost walk under. Archibald was James' younger brother by three years. The two had always been close and when James and his new family left Massachusetts just before medical school, Arch had made his way to central Wisconsin, traveling together to Chicago. He lived, and farmed, a few miles south of Dekorra. He wasn't married and shared the farm with another man he had met on the journey; the two hoped to make enough after a few years to each get his own land. When James had finished at Rush College it was Arch that convinced him to settle and begin a practice in this area.

"Have you given any thought about signing on yourself, James?" Arch asked. The two had spoken a few times recently about joining the militia with James as a surgeon. The past months since Abraham Lincoln's election in November had created a strain on the entire country, a pulling apart by sections like a man being drawn and quartered. The abolitionists in New England couldn't agree with the slaveholders down south or even with the "*Free Soilers*" here in the west. It seemed every part of the Union wanted only their own way; and it wasn't all about slavery either. Tariffs and taxation, rights for free negroes, the questions on how to treat the Indians; all the various issues that could cause dissention between states seemed to be at work. James could easily understand the sudden interest in men wanting to form units to protect the counties and the states; there was more than enough fear to go around.

"Well, Arch, you know I'm the only doctor in the area. It would seem more practical to find one from Madison or another larger town that might have one or two to spare. It's not a question of the money, or the position, or being afraid or anything like that. It's simply that all the people that depend on having a doctor close by...well, they're depending on that staying the same. I couldn't just up and leave if the company was called to the Regular Army. Besides, the Army has their own surgeons, though I'll admit they don't have half enough." James was fighting an inner struggle over this very issue. He considered himself a patriot, ready to answer "the call" of his country; but he could not bring himself to leave the area with no other doctor around.

Just then the door opened and Henry came in. He brightened when he saw his uncle and gave him a hearty handshake, feeling it was the manly thing to do. "Hey Uncle Arch, what are you doing up here in town? Do you have time to go fishing; Marcus caught a huuuuuge pike this morning in the river." Arch looked at his nephew and marveled at how he changed every time they saw each other; the boy must be, what, sixteen now, he thought. Henry was still growing, though he'd probably never reach the height of his uncle. More likely he'd stop at about his dad's five foot ten inches than tower over others like Arch's six foot three.

"Sorry lad, I've no time today. I've got to be getting back to the farm; I'll already be a bit late for the milking. I don't expect Andrew to work my chores every day. James, please see what you may be able to do about getting another doctor into these parts; we could sure use a man we trust with our health." With that, Archibald was gone, out the door as quickly as he came in.

"Hi, Henry; too bad Arch can't go fishing today. I'm feeling like we're going to get real lucky at the river this evening." James looked at his son and watched the face light up like the sun rising. Henry straightened and started for the door. James could hear the "Yiiippppeeee" all the way to the house.

Chapter 2

May 1861

"Well, they've done it. The First Wisconsin is mustered in for three month's service and we're not part of it. They had so many other companies that were already full up; all we can do is keep recruiting and hope we make it into the next regiment." Arch was genuinely disappointed that he wasn't in the first unit to represent the state in the war. Most of the men in the company felt the war would be over before they could even be mustered into a full regiment. The ten companies that formed the First were part of the established state militia and didn't need to add members to reach their full strength. The governor had issued the call for the regiment right after word reached the capital about the *Confederate* attack on Fort Sumter in Charleston, South Carolina. The First had been mustered in for the 90 day period that all the other states were requiring.

James leaned back in his chair on the porch and relaxed. He had felt that Arch had come up to tell him that the local company had been accepted into the First. He was relieved that this was not so. "How many more men do you need to fill up? Do you think you'll be able to get enough to make it into the fight?" he asked. Before Arch could answer Henry and Marcus came up and sat on the steps.

"I don't really know if we'll be able to get the 15 or so more we need. There's always a chance that we could fill up when we get to Camp Randall. That's what they're calling the assembly place down in Madison. I hear they've already got barracks going up and other buildings, too. Seems like a lot of work if this war is as short as they think it will be. I suppose they could use the place later as a new fair site or school or something. Anyway, we're asking everybody we know if they want to join up. Right now it looks like we won't see much fighting anyhow; probably just act as guards somewhere down south when it's over in a month or so. The First should be leaving for Washington in a couple of days and that'll make room for another regiment to gather; we're thinking of going down to Madison the end of the week and offering what we've recruited so far."

"Can't Marcus and I go, too?" Henry asked. "I mean, if it'll be as safe as you say and you'll be there, too, Uncle Arch? "

"Yeah, my pa said he don't mind if I go." Marcus piped up. "'Course, there's plenty more behind me for the folks to care for and I probably won't even be missed. Pa says it might do me some good to learn a little discipline, too." Marcus Dufrense was nearly eighteen, almost two full years older than Henry. The two boys did everything together except go to school; Marcus had stopped going a couple of years earlier. There was no money at all in his family and continuing school made little sense to his folks. His father had lived in Wisconsin his entire life and was the son of a French fur trapper and a Chippewa mother. Marcus had coal black hair and eyes; his freckles came from his mother's side of the family. He was an inch or so taller than Henry and had a similar build; the boys liked to wrestle with each other because they were about the same size and weight. Marcus knew the outdoors like no one else. He would trap, hunt, fish and live outside all year long if he was allowed to. He said it was more comfortable to sleep on the ground than in a bed.

"You know, Marcus, you're nigh on perfect to be a soldier." Arch said. "I don't know why we haven't thought of you before, probably because you're always with Henry and he's only sixteen now."

"Hey, I'm a grown up sixteen!!! Anyway, why can't a sixteen year old my size fight when I'm just as big as Marcus? I hear that you take younger boys in as drummers and such. I don't know how to do that, but I do know how to shoot." Henry was starting to get a bit mad about the whole thing.

"Settle down, son. I'm thinking I'll talk to your mother about this whole thing. For me, the only reason I don't go this minute is that it would leave this area with no doctor. I've written several letters these past weeks but haven't found anyone to come up to take my place so I can go. I think soldiering would fit you for awhile and help get you ready for more school afterward." To James this was not just idle talk; he was seriously working at finding a way to join up himself. Only his duty to his patients kept him from signing right away.

Later that same day Arch met with a few others in the company that also hailed from Dekorra. The topic for discussion at this particular meeting was what to call the unit. Since other companies had already chosen names like "Wisconsin Rifles" and "La Crosse Light Guards", something with a ring to it was called for. It was finally decided that the name "Randall Guards" was fitting, especially since the capital at Madison was located in the same county the company was recruited from. Early the next week Arch and all the others from Dane County assembled at new Camp Randall to muster in and became Company H of the Second Wisconsin. The only real change for them as individuals was the requirement, just announced, that they were volunteering for three years in place of the three months they had originally agreed to. This news did not sit well with everyone and seven men decided to quit, explaining that they couldn't agree to fight this war and not be back home in time to help with the fall harvest.

It was the 16th of the month when the Randall Guards became Company H; the same day Henry and Marcus signed on to join up for three years.

Chapter 3

June 1861

"Hey, Marcus, do you see Colonel Coon over there? He's the one on the bay, in the middle of the three horsemen. Did I tell you that I met him once when my father and I were in Madison? He was high up in the state government then; but I think he's a Democrat. I guess some of them are Union men alright." Henry and his friend were busy sweeping the "street" clean in front of their barrack; the three field officers, Colonel Coon, Lieutenant-Colonel Peck and Major McDonald were riding and inspecting the overall cleanliness of the camp. You could still smell the freshness of the pine boards used to build the barracks and company office. When the First Wisconsin left for Washington a few weeks earlier, they had taken the tents with them. Part of the Second's first instruction was how to build shelters and set up a camp; it seemed the streets were never quite clean enough for the officers.

Now that the camp was finished and the men had been supplied with new militia gray uniforms and equipment, their daily life could best be summed up as "get up, *drill*, march, drill, eat, drill, instruction, drill, eat, march, drill, eat again, drill, drill and a bit more marching before sleep". One day Marcus bet Arch that the company had already marched to the war and they hadn't even left Camp Randall yet. Arch just said to never mind, that this marching was easy since no one was shooting at you.

He explained that all the drill was to make a soldier react automatically to orders; in the confusion of battle a soldier didn't even have to think to follow his instructions. The only way to teach this kind of obedience was to practice it over and over and over. They were learning how to march as a company as well as how to maneuver as an entire regiment. It was a stirring sight to see all 1,000 of them on the parade field during drill. Often there would be hundreds of people from Madison who would come out to watch, especially on Sunday afternoons when the Colonel would call for an inspection after the drilling. The regimental band would play music and the spectators would cheer. Henry and Marcus knew it helped them stand taller and march better; they were taking real pride in their abilities as soldiers. They were also getting anxious to be off to the war so they could beat the Rebels and end the struggle.
It hadn't been all work and no play for the regiment. They also had some fun doing the things new soldiers do; exploring the capital at Madison when they had a few hours with no duty and permission to go. One group practiced laying siege to a brewery; those Germans knew how to put down a foe alright. Henry had even been a part of a funeral for one of the meals a new food contractor provided. The beef was so bad the men decided to formally bury it; they gathered together and led a funeral procession right through camp as a way of protesting the terrible quality of the meat. The Colonel responded by hiring a new food contractor. The men's respect for his leadership grew.

On June 20th the regiment was ordered into formation in front of a new speaker platform on the parade field. The men listened to speeches by their Colonel, the Governor and representatives of various groups from Madison. Then the ladies of Madison presented the regiment with a new silk National flag to carry proudly into battle. The men marched from Camp Randall to the train station and began their journey to Washington by way of Chicago,

Toledo, Cleveland, Pittsburg and Baltimore. At each city they were feasted, toasted and serenaded by the loyal citizens along the way. Marcus and Henry were, of course, most impressed by the young women who came and served them hot coffee and plates of meat, potatoes and fresh pies, cakes and fruit; even hugs and a few kisses. Marcus once said he didn't think there could be so many beautiful girls in the whole world, let alone in just the cities they were passing through. Henry thought on that awhile; he had certainly seen more pretty ones in that week than he had in his whole life. He made himself a promise to not be too quick to settle in Wisconsin when the war was over; he wanted to see a lot more of the country he was fighting to protect.

The regiment arrived in Washington on the 25th and went into camp in one of the suburbs of the capital. At the time it was believed the Confederates were about to attack the city as their army was camped in three locations which almost surrounded Washington. A few days later the regiment was moved across the Potomac River into Virginia to garrison Fort Corcoran, one of the new defense positions being built to protect the city. The Second was *brigaded* with other units under the command of Colonel William T Sherman. During this time only a very few of the men, mostly officers, were allowed to leave camp to explore the area. The majority of the soldiers continued to drill, now in larger units; they were learning the maneuvers necessary to survive on a battlefield.

The tactics of fighting at this time were a carryover from a half century before. Masses of men in straight lines two or more ranks deep would march up to the enemy and stand with no protection within easy musket range and begin to fire volleys. One side or the other would eventually charge with bayonets and take the field and the victory. It was the way battles had been fought for more than a century. With the invention of the rifled musket and improved artillery, these tactics led to wholesale slaughter. A rifled musket could kill at 600 yards compared to the 100 yards of a smoothbore. The common soldier was quick to learn that getting behind cover was the key to survival; it took the senior officers longer to learn the lesson.

It took time as well to learn that outfitting soldiers in similar uniform designs prevented what is now known as "friendly fire". With the Second Wisconsin were other regiments such as the 79th New York, known as the Highlanders. They wore a kilted Scotch dress uniform complete with plaid trousers. Another regiment, the 69th New York, was made up entirely of Irishmen, and carried Kelly green flags emblazoned with the harp of Erin. The 13th New York had one company that went into their first battle complete with black hats and red shirts and coats; they had all been firemen in New York and wore their civilian work clothes. This hodge-podge of colors would only add to the confusion of the early battles about to take place. Naturally, the Second Wisconsin themselves attracted attention due to their gray militia uniforms; although the Seventh New York also wore gray at this time.

Chapter 4

July 1861

"Attention company... By order of the commanding general we are to move out this morning to locate and engage the enemy."

The cheer that followed this command was deafening. At last the fighting was to begin; all of the men had become tired of the drill and inspections that had filled the entire time they had been in the army. They had joined to see action and now, God willing, it's finally to be. Even the newspapers had been full of headlines like "On To Richmond", trying to force the generals to end the war with one decisive blow. General McDowell had been named the commander and, when he tried to explain to President Lincoln that the army was not yet ready to fight, was told "It's true you are green, but they are green as well; you are both green together."

Moving an army of this size not only took a long time, it was also impossible to disguise. Spies in Washington had already informed the Confederate leadership of the Federal intention to attack. Generals Beauregard and Johnston were setting up their defenses to best defeat the Union army.

"Hey, Marcus, look over there. Those New York boys are sending out skirmishers into that orchard; looks like we'll see action soon. I bet we're not even a dozen miles from camp, though we've been two days getting here. I'm already tired from the starting and stopping and not moving we've done. At this rate we won't get to Richmond for a month."

"Henry, I don't think they're skirmishers......unless they're picking the Rebs out of the trees. Look, there's more of them, picking berries along the road ahead. Some fresh blackberries would go down real nice right now but I bet they're all picked out by the time we get up there."

The two could see officers trying to get their men back in ranks to continue the march; but when they saw a New York captain dismount and start to climb a tree to get to the apples, they felt a bit nervous. This march had become more of a pleasure walk than an army on the move. Discipline had never been what they had heard the Regular Army was like; they were volunteers and everyone said strict measures didn't apply to them. How then could officers fall out on the march to pick an orchard clean?

The Second was ordered to take the advance position in the march. They proceeded to Blackburn's Ford on the Bull Run River and were placed in reserve, behind the troops sent to secure this bank of the river. From where they were the men could see the artillery fire from both sides and watched the smoke from the infantry fire drift up and above the woods lining the water's edge. At the end of the day, they marched back to the town of Centreville to make camp for the night. Now the men knew, for certain, that the fighting was just ahead, perhaps in the morning.

Chapter 5

First Bull Run

The sounds of the battle ahead grew louder as the men marched at *route step*. The rattle of muskets fired in volley, sounding like giant bed sheets being torn in two, was complimented by the deep thundering "booms" of the artillery. Yesterday's fight had been a small affair; two men from LaCrosse had been killed and another wounded. Everyone in the ranks believed today would bring a real fight; the smoke clouds covered the horizon from their front all along to the far right. Henry's mouth grew dry with the dust and the anticipation of what lay ahead. He could see Marcus trying to swallow and knew his discomfort was shared by quite a few of his comrades. The men marched along a road through the thick woods and could no longer see the smoke of the battle to their left; but the sounds of it continued. They could hear the ripping noise of a large volley of muskets followed by the shouts of the men attacking. Bullets were beginning to snip off leaves in the trees along their march as they took a left at a fork in the roadway. Soon they were crossing a creek some were calling Bull Run; a few minutes went by and they made another left and Henry realized that Sherman's brigade had just marched around the flank of the fighting and would quickly be in action.

Now the men were forming into a battle line that stretched for almost a half mile, straddling the road they had come in on. The Second Wisconsin was on the far right of the brigade. Ahead they could see a hill with artillery along the crest firing at the troops directly in their front. Over to their right and part way up the hill they watched as another brigade made a charge up toward the big guns. The men marched as if on a practice ground and looked like nothing could stop them. The Second Wisconsin cheered them on as they witnessed the attack. Some of the attackers wore black hats, red shirts and black pantaloons; a man ahead of Henry said they belonged to the First Minnesota, one of the regiments that had signed up to fight months ago. As Henry and Marcus stood and watched, the cannon along the crest of the hill opened up on the troops going up; large gaps formed in the straight lines where the shells exploded and the canister balls tore through the bodies of the Minnesota boys. The regiment stopped and fired a volley before falling back in good order. It had all seemed like a maneuver or a drill; Henry could see many men lying still where the men had stopped to fire. It was the only evidence that this was no practice; those men were dead and dying. Now their own officers were assembling at the front of their brigade; their own colonel was dismounting and drawing his sword. It was their turn to try and take those cannon ahead. Uncle Arch turned around to face Henry and said simply, "Henry.....Marcus.....remember that you are fighting for your home, family and the Union. Make them all proud."

Thirty minutes later they were in the same place, having marched up the hill and back. Henry did not know how many men they had lost; he only knew he was thirstier than he had ever known and that he could not hear anyone that was not shouting at him. The din of the battle blocked out all lesser noise. His head was pounding and he seemed to be choking from all the smoke. The Second had attacked and had even forced the enemy to remove their artillery from the hill. Then more Confederates had come up and the confusion increased as men in a multitude of different uniforms seemed to appear everywhere. Henry later wrote home to say "You just fired your gun as fast as you could load and you kept your eyes on your flag and officers." When they were ordered to fall back they did so with a pride and precision that drew the attention of their commanding general.

That night the Second marched up the roads back to Washington. None of the men wore the discouragement or desperation that was so evident in most of the army. Though the battle had ended in a southern victory, the Wisconsin men felt they had handled the fighting and endured the marching well. Henry was still troubled by the ringing in his ears and often had to remind his uncle and Marcus to speak louder. The last few miles to their camp outside of the capital were the longest Henry had ever walked; the rain that had soaked them during most of the retreat had now become a torrent and the roads were ankle deep in mud. The following days were also full of confusion. Rumors of an impending Confederate attack on Washington caused senior officers to issue conflicting orders to move or entrench or stand to their arms or prepare to retreat across the Potomac River. The men were all on edge and irritable; there were several fistfights over things that usually wouldn't bother them at all. The only positive thing that happened during the week concerned their uniforms. Because of the confusion caused by the color of the Wisconsin's militia clothing they wore, new outfits of Federal dark blue coats and light blue trousers were issued. From this day on, with the exception of some rather flamboyant *Zouave* units, the northern army would all wear blue; the southern *seccesh* would be in gray or variations of butternut.

Chapter 6

July 1861

Dearest Mother and Father,

I'm writing this letter from our camp just across the Potomac River from Washington. We have been in a large battle which we hear was not a victory for our side, though our officers tell us we behaved well. Uncle Arch and Marcus are both fine as I am also. I have a hard time hearing out of one ear though I think it is getting better. The noise of the battle we fought along Bull Run Creek cannot be imagined. You could see the men's mouths moving without hearing their words even if they stood right beside you. All I could hear was the sounds of the muskets and cannon and the angry buzzing of bullets going by. It seemed like hours that we stood and fought against others dressed in the same colors we wore; we were even shot at by some on our side. So now we've been given blue uniforms so we shall not be seen as Rebels again. I've heard we lost about 20 boys in the Second but have not read or heard of any that I knew at home being killed. Uncle and Marcus and I have counted a total of seven holes in our own blouses from enemy fire. I guess we were too busy to notice them during the fight. Being in a real battle is not what I thought it would be, but now we have *seen the elephant* as they say here and will know better what to do if we have to fight again. Your loving son, Henry McCollum

Marcus had just left to go find a *sutler* where he could post the letters back to Wisconsin. Henry was sitting at the fire in front of their tent drinking a very hot cup of coffee. Arch ambled up, took a seat on a cracker box and pulled out his pipe. Opening a leather pouch of tobacco he packed the bowl of the pipe and lit it with a small stick from the fire. After a few puffs, Arch stretched and pointed the stem at Henry. "You know, Henry, what we went through yesterday is something most people will never experience in their lives, no matter how long that life is. To take part in a great battle and to come out of it alive is, perhaps, the greatest thing a man can do. You and Marcus were real men in that fight. I know how proud your father would be right here, right now because it is precisely how I feel. Others your age back home may be called "boy" by the older men in town, but that is something you two have outgrown now." Arch moved to the ground, leaning back against the cracker box and stretched his long frame, looked at the sunset beginning to color the western sky and let out a long slow sigh.

Henry was sitting, reflecting on the words and praise his uncle had just uttered. He did not really feel any different than he had before the battle, though he was thankful for getting through the fight safely. As Marcus ambled up to the fire from posting the letters, he immediately sensed the sober atmosphere; he sat down and quietly began gathering the tools needed to clean his musket. Marcus had spent much of the afternoon with one of the former regulars in the regiment who was helping him become a better marksman. It seemed the young man had a natural ability at the varied skills it took to make a great soldier; it was a direct benefit derived from the way he had been raised back in the woods of Wisconsin.

Chapter 7

Fall / Winter 1861

The changes in the army happened quickly, though to Henry and Marcus the days seemed full of routine. A new army commander, General George McClellan, was appointed to organize, train and better equip the northern troops. They were now called the Army of the Potomac and the men learned to greatly admire their new commanding general. He would often be seen riding, followed by a large group of his staff officers. He was called "Little Mac" by the troops and he had promised them they would not fight again until he felt they were ready. The regiments were organized into new brigades, the brigades into divisions and the divisions into corps. Officers were instructed daily in what they were expected to know and to do; those that could not, or would not, perform were slowly weeded out. Camps were better organized and the men were drilled constantly on everything required of them. Large reviews of the troops were held, often involving thousands of soldiers marching across a field; often they were paraded in front of important people from Washington, even President Lincoln came to watch several times. The men became more confident and proud of their army.

But there was little fighting. In the fall, part of the army was sent across the Potomac in search of the Rebels at a place called Ball's Bluff. It was another disaster. The commanders assigned by Little Mac proved to be less than able at their jobs. It seemed the best officers were in the Confederate Army. Newspapers began to question General McClellan's ability to command, asking what good a large army was if it wasn't used to fight. Most of his soldiers felt differently; they loved their General for not just sending them into a fight without everything being ready. The weather turned colder and the army was told to prepare for winter.

Henry, Marcus and Archibald began to dig; first a square, about seven feet on a side and two feet deep. The dirt was carefully piled up on each side of the square leaving a space that would become their doorway on the south side. Arch said they were lucky to have gotten the north side of the "street" as the winter sun would still shine in the opening and help warm them later. After the walls of dirt were packed, they used their tent panels to make a pitched roof over their hut. One of the former regulars, Sergeant Major Spear, from LaCrosse, told them how to make a chimney and fireplace in the hut. They took three salt pork barrels without ends, stacked them up and used mud to cement them together. This just reached above the top of their roof to allow for the wind to draw the fire. They used rocks and more mud to make the hearth inside the hut. With simple beds, and a table fashioned out of cracker boxes and straw mattresses, their new home would be snug and dry. A man could just barely stand up in the hut; Arch, of course, was never able to. Henry and Marcus kidded him constantly about his height. They said they'd need at least two more barrels to make a chimney tall enough to accommodate the roof he required.

The brigade made quite a neat village; they even built a church for Sunday services and a bakery for fresh bread. The rows of huts were straight with swept dirt streets; the regiments were housed with each company in its own neighborhood. The men resumed their drill, but with more time for writing letters, reading, cards and other distractions. That winter, the newspapers in the north made a joke out of the expression “All quiet along the Potomac”.

Chapter 8

Spring 1862

"What I don't understand is why we have to Rebuild this danged fence. If we had been the ones that took and burned it, alright; but we didn't. It was those blasted Hoosiers in the 19th Indiana that did. I saw them last night sneaking over and coming back with the rails." Marcus was sweating, even though it was still chilly in the spring morning. He and Henry had been assigned the job of cutting new rails for the fence that had "gone up in smoke" the night before. "I heard it's the orders of the new brigade commander, you know, we saw him yesterday when he rode past. Uhhhhh, Gibbon, that's it. General John Gibbon, used to be the captain of Battery B. Now there's a nice bunch of boys; why do you suppose he'd go from being in a great bunch like that to making innocent men work like this?

Henry was struggling to lift a log onto the supports to start splitting it with the wedges and mallet. He'd heard that President Lincoln used to split rails when he was about his own age down in Illinois where he grew up. Henry liked the thought of a leader knowing what it was like to work this hard. As for General Gibbon....the boys he'd talked to said he was a Regular officer through and through; he'd put up with no fooling around. He was all "straight and tight" when it came to soldiering. Henry had heard that Gibbon was from North Carolina and had three brothers who were all Confederate officers. While others spoke badly about that, Henry thought it must be hard on a man to see his family split apart like this.

One thing was for sure; he'd be getting a lot stronger real quick if he kept building fences across the state of Virginia.

John Gibbon was, in fact, from North Carolina. He was also completely dedicated to the Union and its preservation. It had cost him his family, but he considered it a fair price. To him, this country was what the entire world needed; freedom to become your own success or failure, not your father's or anyone else's. He had been patient with the delay in his getting a star; there were no Senators or Congressmen to support him. They had all left Washington when his home state seceded; but a couple of northern politicians had taken his side and Congress had finally approved his promotion. He was glad to have his old Battery B back under his command. He knew their quality and hoped the Wisconsin and Indiana volunteers he now led would have similar character. He sensed they were smart men, confident in their own abilities; he had heard this was a trademark of the westerners. "A very independent lot" he had been told. He hoped it was true; he planned to make them the best brigade in the whole Army of the Potomac!

"So now we have to get different uniforms again? I was just getting used to the blue; what color now.....red like the blasted English? And, no doubt, we'll have to buy them from our own money?" Corporal McAhern was not at all pleased at the new orders. Sergeant Major Spear had just informed the other non-coms of General Gibbon's instructions. The regiment, along with the others in the brigade, was to be outfitted with a uniform normally reserved for Regular Army troops.

The new uniform consisted of a dark blue frock coat, longer than the sack coat the volunteers wore. It reached nearly to the knees and was buttoned up to the throat. It was also trimmed with sky blue piping around the collar, cuffs and down the front. The regular sky blue pants would remain, although the men would also wear white leggings and, for parade and dress, white cotton gloves. The most significant, and visible, change was the headgear. In place of the regular kepi or forage cap, worn by the vast majority of eastern troops, the brigade would wear the regulation 1858 hat known as the Hardee. It was very tall, like a stovepipe, with a wide brim turned up on the left side and dressed with a black ostrich plume on the right. A blue tasseled hatcord was also worn along with the brass "hunting horn" infantry device. It was certainly an impressive looking uniform, but in the eyes of the volunteers it was almost totally impractical. Nevertheless, orders are orders and General Gibbon wanted his brigade to stand out from the rest. Each soldier would also adorn the front of the hat with the regimental number and company letter for easy identification.

Two weeks later a package arrived at the McCollum home in Dekorra. It contained a letter from Henry along with a *tintype* picture of him in his new uniform; his bright eyed round face staring intently and proud in the stiff necked frock coat with the Hardee hat perched on his head. There was just a hint of jauntiness in the tilt of the hat over to one side. Henry had posted the package immediately after the tintype was made by a photographer that had passed through the army camps. It was the only picture he had ever sat for; Arch had one taken as well and it was also included. Mail service to and from the front was about the only way to stay connected as a family and the government made sure it worked well.

"How long we been marching today? I wish they'd kill us off in battle rather than march us to death like pack mules." Henry was struggling to keep up; Arch's long legs seemed to be having an easier time of the pace. They had been on the road since before sunup and the heat and humidity of the day had caused hundreds of the men to throw away their heavy packs and winter overcoats along the road. Knowing that Rebel cavalry would scoop them up and use them only made it worse. The brigade was used to being garrison soldiers, staying pretty much in one place. Now here they were hot-footing it through Virginia trying to beat Confederate general Stonewall Jackson's "foot cavalry" to the town of Front Royal. Jackson had been in the north end of the Shenandoah Valley and the Union army now had a chance to trap him as he headed back south, but they had to hurry. Jackson's forces always traveled light and relied on captured Federal supplies, like the overcoats no longer being carried by the boys in blue.

The Second Wisconsin finally stopped at sundown; they had marched a hard twenty miles that day, marking the end of their first year in the army. As the men pitched their tents, dozens of stragglers managed to make it into camp. These men had fallen out from exhaustion along the march and faced the prospect of being captured if they didn't find their own lines before nightfall. Henry and Marcus crawled into their tent, looking forward to a much anticipated rest when Corporal McAhern leaned in and told them they would be part of the skirmishers for the regiment in the morning. They would have to get up well before dawn as the brigade would be advancing to Front Royal, now only a couple miles ahead.

Henry was moving through the brush, careful to keep low, along with the other skirmishers. The early morning dew had already soaked his legs and his *brogans* were just beginning to make that squish sound. The sun was up, maybe a thumb above the horizon ahead, making it harder to look into its brightness. He was, perhaps, fifteen yards from the edge of a small wooded patch when the Rebel stood up ahead of him, rifled musket already aimed at his chest. Henry dropped the barrel of his Springfield a bit and pulled the trigger, the gun bucked as it went off. He expected to feel the punch of a ball into his body; looking through the smoke he saw that his shot had hit the Reb right in his hand at the trigger of his own rifle, causing him to drop it. Henry ran at the enemy, reversing his grip to club his musket, wheeling it at the man's head.

The Confederate dropped down, sliding just under the swinging stock, and pulled a short knife out of his belt. Henry saw the flash of the sun on the blade less than an inch from his eyes and tasted the warm saltiness of blood. His musket had slipped from his hands as he swung it, the result of the wet grass he'd been in. He reached for his own knife and remembered it was back at camp; he dove at his opponent as the man was starting another wide arc with the knife. The two bodies collided and rolled over and over, the blade flashing in the sunlight. Henry felt the weight of the bigger man on him as they slid down an embankment into the cold wetness of a creek bottom. The man had his fingers in Henry's mouth, trying to wrench his head around; he bit down hard and felt the fingers break, like chicken bones. Letting out a pain filled yell, the man straightened just a bit and gave Henry the moment he needed. He had already felt the rough surface of the rock as his hand scrambled to find something, anything, to use as a weapon. Now his arm came up quickly and the rock's edge caught the man squarely on the side of the head. The blood shot out in a spray and the Rebel went limp, his weight falling hard on Henry. All he could do was lay there a minute, catching his breath, waiting for his heart to get back down in his chest.

He wriggled out from under the dead man, not wanting to look at him. In a brief moment, he thanked God he had won; then he turned, looked at the body and let out his own yell. It was a primal scream of triumph and relief, and was followed by Henry bending over and vomiting into the creek.

"What in heaven's name happened to your face?" Arch was horrified when he saw Henry being helped by another man. The tip of his nose had been cut off during the fight and the blood of both fighters had combined to make quite a picture. The bleeding had stopped for now and Henry's whole body seemed to be hurting; he had never felt this sore in his entire life. He had already discovered that the end of his nose was missing, but he had no idea what he looked like. His uncle's expression told him much, he must look frightful; right now he wanted to wash up and survey the damage for himself. He was also incredibly tired.

Chapter 9

Summer 1862

His nose had pretty well healed, though now it was a bit shorter. His uncle and Marcus joked that it would be more difficult for him to stick it into other people's business. Henry went along with the ribbing and was confident that he could take care of himself in a fight. Following the failure to spring a trap on Stonewall Jackson and his army, the brigade had returned to the area around the Rappahannock River near Fredericksburg. The men were tired of all the marching they had done; at the same time most agreed that they had learned much about traveling light and fast as infantry. Though they had not been involved in any real fighting since Bull Run a year ago, there was a growing awareness that it was only a matter of time until the Western troops would be called upon to pitch in once more.

Most of the Army of the Potomac, under General McClellan, was now in an area known as the Peninsula, bounded by the York and the James rivers. Within a few miles of Richmond, the Federals were halted by vicious Confederate attacks. Over a period of seven days the Rebels, under newly appointed commander General Robert E Lee, drove McClellan's army back, forcing him to suspend the planned attack on the southern capital city. Immediately afterward, Lee seized the opportunity of destroying a large portion of the Union forces protecting Washington as the Army of the Potomac remained on the Peninsula licking its wounds.

"So Arch, what do you know of this new general, Pope? I hear he's all hellfire and damnation, he's come from out west where they only see the backsides of the Rebs." Marcus was acting all puffed up, strutting like a rooster in a chicken yard.

"I'll say this to you, young bantam; no general yet that's gone around crowing has shown his real spurs in combat. So far all I've heard of is their noise and then the whimper as they fade away when the Johnnies arrive. I don't think this General Pope will be any different than McDowell or his lot; all talk and no action." Arch was busy tamping his pipe, filled with delicious southern tobacco he had gotten the night before when he was on *picket* duty down at the river.

The Yank and Rebel soldiers got to be rather friendly when the officers weren't around; often they would trade newspapers for books, or tobacco for coffee. Yesterday Henry had even posted a letter to New York for a North Carolina private. The two had talked for several minutes and Henry learned the man was actually a cousin of General Gibbon and was writing to another relative up north. The next several hours found Henry thinking about their encounter; he thought it was strange how friendly it had all been, natural almost, for the two enemies to talk and trade. Only a few short weeks ago he had killed another man quite like this one; that meeting had not been nearly as pleasant. Henry came back to his tent after his guard duty convinced that war was a terribly strange thing indeed.

"Is this just another goose chase like our march up to Front Royal? We've been going most of the day with no time to fall out and rest. There have already been more than a dozen of our guys that have collapsed; how many more?" Arch was talking with Sergeant Bennett of A

Company, whose first name happened to be Arch as well. “You know” said Bennett, “I’m not sure who ordered this march, but if we happen to catch Jackson this time, we’ll be too tuckered out to do anything with him. I’d be more willing to wear my legs down to the knees if I knew that Stonewall Brigade was at the end of this hike.”

There was the blast of two cannon ahead and to the left, beyond a small wood they were marching by. Officers on horseback galloped past and, up ahead, the Sixth Wisconsin was beginning to move off the road and into line of battle. Sergeant Bennett bid farewell to Arch and began to move quickly ahead, to catch up with his company. Henry and Marcus moved closer as Arch said “Well, boys, it looks like we may have found old Stonewall at last.”

The men were formed into line of battle after they had marched back to the edge of the wood. In the clear ground leading up to some buildings on the top of the shorter rise they could see the smoke from a couple more Rebel cannon. General Gibbon had ordered the Second Wisconsin to move up the ridge and drive off, or capture, the enemy guns. The entire brigade of four regiments numbered about 2,100 men. As the Second advanced quietly up the slope with skirmishers deployed forward, the men began to feel confident they could get close enough to the guns for one final rush and capture them. Suddenly Rebel infantry appeared, coming from behind the farm buildings ahead and to the right. Quickly they formed into line and fired a volley into the right flank of the Yankees. Colonel O’Connor went down with a bullet in his thigh along with several other men. Major Allen ordered a right oblique to face the enemy and the Wisconsin men let go their first volley. It ripped into the Confederates; one man was to comment later how, after the smoke had cleared, the enemy looked more like a skirmish line than an entire regiment.

Henry and Arch were in the middle of the Second's line, loading and firing faster than they had ever practiced. The late afternoon sun was hot, the gunpowder from biting the end off the cartridges coated their lips, mouths were so dry no water helped, and their ears were ringing from all the noise. Fire, load, fire, load.....all the while men were falling, spinning around, blood flying, arms flailing, screaming. One man to the right of Henry was laughing hysterically as he loaded and pulled the trigger, never *capping* the musket. After he had loaded perhaps four times he remembered a percussion cap; when he pulled the trigger the barrel of his rifle exploded and blew off most of his face. He screamed once and fell.

Marcus was with the skirmishers when the Rebs came out from behind the farm house. He managed to get off one shot before he felt the burning sting of a ball as it hit his leg. The bone had not completely shattered and he found he could still stand. Loading his gun he was aiming it at an officer on a horse when the second bullet hit him in the same leg a few inches higher. As he went down he spun to face down the slope and rolled over and over until he stopped in a small depression. Bullets whipped through the grass and threw up dirt all around him; they sounded like giant bees as they flew past. He couldn't see anything up the hill but could watch as, below him, the main line of the Second seemed to slowly melt into the ground. He knew they could not stay there and survive long.

The fight went on and on for over two hours. Men had long ago rummaged through the cartridge boxes of the wounded and dead to find another round to load and fire. Still the entire brigade stood and fought. From left to right the 19th Indiana, Second and Seventh Wisconsin, reinforcements from the 56th Pennsylvania and 76th New York, and the Sixth Wisconsin battled Jackson's men. Stonewall continued to pour in more and more men until there were more than 6,400 Confederates facing less than 3,000 Yanks. Neither side could advance and neither would retreat.

As the sun set and darkness settled in, the two lines were still firing though fewer men were being hit. Finally General Gibbon ordered the Black Hats to fall back around and through the woods to the road behind them. They had to leave the dead and wounded behind. The Rebels followed them only a short distance and then they, too, fell back to their original position on the far side of the ridge. Now the northerners went back up the hill a ways to try and gather up the wounded. Small clearings in the woods soon were filled with the moaning and crying of those who had been hit. Marcus had managed to drag himself along to a point where he was found by some Indiana men and they took him to their regimental surgeon. There was nothing much that could be done for him here; Marcus was put on one of the only wagons available along with many other wounded, stacked up like cord wood for the long, slow ride to Manassas Junction where a hospital was being set up.

Henry and Arch both managed to come through the fight without a scratch. Neither of them had time to take note of the amazing quality of that; they were busy lifting and carrying the wounded into the woods. Around midnight those men who were able to march, including wounded, started along the road to Manassas. Some held on to horse's stirrups, others were helped by comrades. Arch would always remember it as the longest night he ever experienced. The two wondered about Marcus but had no chance to find him or any news of him. Both believed that he had been killed early on along with most of the other skirmishers. They marched along, taking small sips of water to conserve what little they had. It was still dark when they arrived at the railroad junction and heard the order to fall out and get some rest. As the weary officers arranged for some food to be brought, Henry, Arch and the rest of the Second lay down where they stood . . . in the road. None of them had the energy to move anywhere before they fell asleep.

As the sun rose, quickly burning off the light dew, it promised to be another hot and dusty day. Henry and Arch woke to the smell of hundreds of small fires and boiling coffee. The brigade was spread alongside the road, though after yesterday's fight it didn't spread nearly as long. Henry's body was incredibly stiff and he felt as if his bones would break if he stretched too much. His first thoughts were of Marcus; he had last seen his friend before the firing started and had no idea where he was. He asked his uncle to please try to learn any news about Marcus while he started some coffee and prepared a small breakfast of hardtack and fried pork. Arch said he'd try and started off to find their company officers.

The coffee was just beginning to boil and the pork was half cooked when he returned to tell Henry that he had not been able to learn much; no one had seen Marcus once the fight began. What Arch did learn was that not a single man from the skirmishers had returned to the regiment during the night. He also was told that nearly two out of every three of the brigade's soldiers were casualties; killed, wounded or missing. While they were talking the sound of the long roll on the drums was heard. Immediately the men of the Second began to gather their equipment, put out the small cooking fires, grabbed their food and moved to fall into ranks.

The brigade was on the road, retracing their march from last night. Henry was hopeful they would be able to locate Marcus somewhere ahead, perhaps in the woods where he had helped move wounded the evening before. Before they reached the area surrounding the Brawner Farm, artillery fire was heard off towards the right of their march. Not far from the scene of yesterday's fight the brigade was halted and ordered to protect the reserve artillery as other troops again assaulted Jackson's lines, which were well protected by the ridge and railroad cut on the other side.

During the afternoon news of the wounded and missing began to filter in to the men of the Second Wisconsin as they remained along a slightly higher position near Henry House Hill. It was very near to the area they had first fought the Confederates just over a year ago in the first battle along Bull Run creek. It seemed that soon, perhaps tomorrow, another large battle would take place here. Henry grew anxious about Marcus; some of the other skirmishers had been located but they knew nothing of what had happened to him. Arch had spoken with some members of the 19th Indiana who had moved several wounded Wisconsin men into their doctors' area in the woods the night before; no one knew any names but one man remembered a young, dark haired soldier badly wounded in the leg. The McCollums determined to speak with the Indiana doctors as soon as they could. Meanwhile, the brigade was ordered to sleep *on their arms* that night, the men not getting much rest while lying with their packs on and rifles in their hands.

Most of the next day was spent by the Union commander, General John Pope, adjusting his lines to best attack General Jackson's position. Pope had assumed that the Rebels were retreating. In reality, General Lee had arrived with General Longstreet's *corps* to reinforce Jackson's line. The Yankees were marching to attack with a large enemy force on their left flank and they didn't know it. The Second Wisconsin was now almost in the middle of the entire Union position, still assigned to protect the reserve artillery. Henry had found time that morning to speak with the Indiana men; all he learned was that the Hoosier doctors had moved their hospital along with the brigade the first night. Marcus, if he had been with them, would be back near where they had slept on the road soon after the Brawner Farm fight. There was no opportunity for Henry to find him until after the upcoming fight ended.

The brigade came out of some woods in line of battle and ran into a hailstorm of lead and iron; Longstreet's artillery poured shot and shell in from the left. As the fire came in along the length of the Union lines, there was little chance of not hitting someone. From their front the Confederate infantry was firing from behind the railroad embankment, backed up by cannon firing canister, those small round iron balls that cleared whole swaths through the lines. Henry, along with the men of the other regiments, pulled his hat down tight and leaned into the storm; it was very much like walking into a heavy rain, except these drops were deadly.

To the left they could hear the Rebel yell above the noise of the battle; soon there were other Federal troops running, scared out of their minds, through their lines. The western men remained cool under the enemy attack, reforming and facing the new threat. They became the rear guard; holding off the Confederates while the rest of Pope's army began retreating over the old battlefield and along the same roads some of them had taken back to Washington a year earlier. Once again it turned into a *skedaddle*, seeing who would get back to the safety of the capital first. As Henry and the rest of the Second Wisconsin marched through the night rain, keeping the Rebels at bay, he gave up all thought of finding Marcus here in Virginia. He now set his mind on searching the Washington hospitals for his friend.

Chapter 10

South Mountain

Two days after reaching their old camp outside Washington the brigade was, again, getting ready to move. Henry could not believe things could move so fast in the army; at least they never had before. New officer appointments for the regiments to replace so many that had been killed or seriously wounded in the fighting around Bull Run had been immediately followed by new equipment and a replenishment of ammunition for the western troops. General McClellan had been put back in command of the entire Army of the Potomac and the brigade was assigned to the First Corps. General Gibbon was a good friend of Little Mac and he received a promise that the brigade would be assigned the first available western regiment to build up their strength. After the fight at Brawner's Farm and Second Manassas the brigade was below 1,000 men.

"I tell you, Uncle, I'm going to be tying my shoes above the knees if we have another march like yesterday. I hear tell we moved some twenty seven miles!!!" Henry was adjusting his bedroll and fastening it to his pack as the men were beginning to fall in for another long march. Thankfully, it was a cool morning and the rain overnight would help keep the dust down. Even though it added weight, Henry had acquired an extra canteen and he made sure it was full; he knew it would come in handy later in the day. The regiment was to head west and north in pursuit of Lee's Army of Northern Virginia. After beating Pope the week before, Lee had ordered his army north; he hoped to accomplish much. He believed many men would join his army in Maryland, a former slave state; he also felt that another military victory, especially in the north, would bring England and France into the war on the south's side. These ideas were far above the minds of soldiers like Arch and Henry. They only knew the enemy was ahead and had to be dealt with.

"Henry, I want you to know I wrote a couple of letters yesterday and got them posted just before we left this morning. One is to your folks and the other to the governor of Wisconsin. I've asked that they help however they can in locating Marcus. There have been way too many boys just disappear in this war; we don't need our friend to be another." Henry knew that his father would do whatever it took to locate Marcus. There was no time for a couple of soldiers to look at all the hospitals in the capital trying to find one wounded man. It just seemed strange that Marcus had not been able to get in touch with them; it made Henry worry more, thinking how bad he must be hurt.

Later that day the two could hear the church bells of Frederick, Maryland, as they marched closer to the town. They had put in more than twenty miles today and the marching was hard; in the western brigade there was almost no straggling; General Gibbon had instilled a sense of pride in the unit they had not known before. Now it was almost an honor to not fall out along the way instead of thinking of a way to quit. The men would even jeer and poke fun at the stragglers from other units. Yes, sir, the western Black Hat Brigade was making a name for itself.

As they entered Frederick, Gibbon himself pulled the brigade off the road and gathered them in an empty area. He spoke to them about the coming fight; the opportunity to beat the Confederates, the need for a couple more days of hard marching and the news that a new Michigan regiment would soon join them. The men cheered that they would remain the only entirely western brigade in the eastern army. For now they would get a few hours rest just outside the town…

The next day General Gibbon reported to General McClellan; the orders were to advance the brigade along the National Road toward the summit of South Mountain. The Rebels had blocked all three passes over the high ground the army had to cross to reach Hagerstown where the main Confederate forces were located. Brigades from other corps would march up and attack the southern positions at the two outside passes; Gibbon's brigade was to go straight up the National Road and attack the forces holding the middle. As usual, Gibbon's old command, Battery "B" of the Second US Artillery would provide support in breaking through the Rebel entrenchments.

Henry and Arch had fallen in with the rest of the company and were marching up the road toward the summit of the mountain, past the two guns of the battery that would fire over their heads in support. The sun was already dropping in the western sky; like the fight at Brawner Farm, this one would take start in the twilight and continue into the darkness. There were thick woods on the mountain, broken up now and then by small farms and an occasional rock wall dividing the land.

Henry moved automatically, like it wasn't really him but someone else and he was just watching from somewhere up above. He knew what was coming; it would be another rainstorm of iron and lead. The Second left the road and continued through a field as Rebel cannon fire began to cut through the treetops on their way to seek out the big guns behind them. A minute later they could begin to see muzzle flashes of muskets clutched in the hands of equally determined men; only these men wanted him dead.

From behind some of those rock walls that ran through the woods Confederate troops were laying down a pretty good fire on the boys in blue. A man to Henry's right threw his hands to his face as if he could catch the bullet that had already gone through his brain, spraying the men behind him. Henry barely glanced at him, his mind already shutting down anything that didn't lead him through the madness of the night. The company continued to work its way toward the wall ahead; as they neared it the Rebels could just be seen backing away, then turning and running through the brush and trees, like ghosts. Now the Yanks moved faster, their fingers itching to pull triggers. Arch paused only an instant, brought his musket up and fired. A man about ten yards ahead, just visible, threw out his arms as the bullet hit him square in the back, between his shoulders. Arch was already reloading on the run, a difficult thing to do even in the brightness of a day. And so it went on……

Chapter 11

September 1862

Henry awoke from the smell of bacon frying. He lay still with his eyes closed. He imagined he was alongside the Chippewa River back home and could almost hear the gentle swishing of the water as it flowed over the smooth black rocks. The birds began their morning songs as if to hurry the sun on its way up. A crow cawed and the other birds near it hushed for just an instant then continued with their own sweeter sounds. Henry waited in the warmth of his blanket, slowly stretching to work out the stiffness of a deep sleep. He could almost hear his friend's voice whispering that the fish were waiting to be caught. He rubbed his face and felt......the stub of his nose. In an instant the river and his friend's voice disappeared, replaced by the reality of the battlefield. He knew what he would see outside his tent; the dozens of others of what was left of the Second Wisconsin after yesterday's fight. But the smell of that bacon just would not go away.

"Good mornin' lad." Uncle Arch poked his head into Henry's view. "I rustled up some real bacon, wish we had more than crackers to go with it; I dreamed of a few good fresh hen's eggs. Well, maybe tomorrow."

Henry stirred and crawled out of the tent. The stiffness of a good sleep paled in comparison with what he felt; his whole body screamed at him in protest over every movement. He remembered, in a sort of fog, that they had been given the tents of the regiment that had replaced them on the mountain top after the fight ended late in the night. Now he began to recall the confusion and noise and fear, all multiplied by the darkness, the stumbling over rocks as they went up the hill, Rebel artillery and musket fire taking men out on either side of him. Henry knew that as long as he lived, the sound of a bullet striking a body and the crumpling sound as the man fell would never leave his ears.

"Bacon's done; coffee's ready....you gonna have a bite or sit there with your head sideways all morning?" Arch handed him a plate piled with the bacon and two crackers. He set a steaming tin mug of very black, very hot coffee at his feet. Henry shook his head hard, clearing the images of last night from his mind. I'll think on that later, maybe.....

Their meal was nearly complete when the *long roll* was beaten out by the drummers. They would be on the move again today. Arch dumped the tin pot of coffee on the fire and stirred the embers to put them out. Henry packed his gear and in less than two minutes both had fallen in ranks for the start of a new day's march. Now that the sun was up they both could see just how few men were left in the regiment. The entire brigade numbered fewer than 1,000 men; the number the Second had started with back in Madison when they were first formed. It was sad.

Because the brigade had fought alone the night before, they had to march through the units of the Second Corps to reach the camps of their own, the First Corps. As they marched ahead, the men were surprised to hear the cheers of the men of the Second Corps whose own commander, General Sumner, had agreed that the westerners deserved to be recognized for their abilities demonstrated in the fight for South Mountain.

"I can't help thinking about Marcus. Why is it nobody can find out where he is? I'm beginning to think he's been captured by the Rebels." Henry was speaking with Arch as they marched over the summit and began the long downhill trudge to the valley below. As they passed one farmhouse a man was standing on a large rock shouting his thanks for the arrival of the Union troops; the men cheered him as they passed. The mood of the soldiers improved with each mile they marched; each group of civilians they went by would approach the ranks handing out fresh milk, bread, pies and other treats. Young women came up with flowers, often delivered with a kiss. These people had heard of the Black Hats and their fight for the summit.

As they marched through the valley word was passed along the ranks of a conversation between their own commanding generals after the struggle for South Mountain. It was said that General "Fighting Joe" Hooker himself had referred to them as his "Iron Brigade". Every one of the men agreed the name was one that would stick; the only all western unit in the entire Army of the Potomac deserved a special name. From this moment they were, forever, the Iron Brigade.

"I was talking with some of the Company A lads and it's true. Colonel Fairchild has been replaced by Colonel Allen. They say Fairchild is about used up, he could hardly mount and ride this morning." Arch was lighting his pipe as Henry was speaking. They had been given a few minutes to rest on the march. Henry had, again, gone to try to get information on Marcus. None of the other skirmishers from the fight at Brawner's Farm were around either.

"Well, Colonel Allen is a fine man. He will do us proud I'm sure. It appears we'll be marching another couple of hours; I've heard the Rebs are at a place called Sharpsburg up ahead. It looks like more fighting for the Iron Brigade....brigade, to be sure, we don't have enough men left to make more than a couple of companies all together. Well, I hope we can find some berry bushes or an orchard up ahead; we'll be needing the food. I'm thinking we've outrun the supply wagons, they're probably on the other side of South Mountain still." Henry had to be thankful for Arch, he was always thinking ahead.

Less than an hour later, marching at the front of the First Corps column, the Wisconsin men were able to strip most of the apples from an orchard they marched through. A mile further was a cornfield just waiting to be picked clean. With full haversacks and enjoying sweet, juicy apples the men continued at route step, covering the miles with a new energy they hadn't felt all day. Two hours later they passed over Antietam Creek on a bridge near a farm belonging to a family named Pry. When they had reached the other side, Rebel artillery boomed ahead and the brigade was told to halt in a ravine that protected them from the enemy shells. "No rest for the weary. I'm sure there will be 'hell to pay' in the morning", Arch sighed and pulled out his pipe.

Chapter 12

Antietam

He awoke to a light rain and damp, the same rain that had tormented his attempt at sleep during the night. They had been ordered to sleep in line with their guns at the ready. The brightening sky in the east was barely visible when the popping of skirmishers' fire began. It started with one, then two, then a handful, then dozens along their front; each side was feeling out the other, trying to discern just where the enemy lines were in the dark and fog and cold wetness. The day that would become the deadliest single one in American history began with one nervous skirmisher pulling a trigger.

The Iron Brigade was ordered to the front of Hooker's First Corps, to begin the attack by breaking through the Confederate's left and gaining the higher ground beyond the Hagerstown Pike road. From the Poffenberger Farm where they formed into line the westerners were under Rebel rifle and artillery fire causing gaps, small and large, in their formation. Henry knew what to do, sidestepping to his right to fill the gaps. Soon they approached the Miller Farm and ahead could be seen a cornfield. Above the stalks of ripening corn was the glint of Confederate bayonets in the early sunshine. Looking to his right, Henry could see the entire Brigade as it advanced; his own Second, then the Sixth divided in two parts by the pike, then the Seventh Wisconsin and finally the 19th

Indiana. It didn't seem like a very long line at all considering it was a brigade front.

The shot and shell of Battery B was going over them and landing in the corn, throwing up dirt, stalks, arms, legs and an occasional haversack. The sounds of the wounded and dying Henry knew were there couldn't carry over their own shouting and the noise of the Rebel shells landing amongst themselves. As Henry looked around he saw the grim determination on faces; Arch turned his head and shouted to be heard. "Stay by me, lad. Today will be a hot one again."

Now they were in the corn, advancing through the stalks higher than his head. Henry couldn't see more than four feet to the front. Bringing his musket down through the growth was nearly impossible and the advance slowed to a crawl. The dust and smoke made his eyes and lungs burn. The noise was unbelievable; he imagined that hell itself could not be any worse. The man on Henry's right took a bullet in the face and crumpled to the ground, his place taken by another from the rear rank. Henry felt the tug on his coat and the burn as a ball grazed his upper arm; he didn't bother to look. A shell exploded above them and three more men near him went down. This was the worst he had known; an unseen enemy killing them as they struggled through the high corn. Henry could see a slight brightness ahead and knew they were nearly out of the field.

As they came out of Miller's corn field, the men could see a line of Confederates behind a fence fifty or so yards ahead. A cloud of smoke issued from the enemy ranks just as Arch screamed "Down, lad, now". As Henry dropped, out of the corner of his eye he saw nearly the entire first rank of men go down, arms flailing, rifles dropping. The last three weeks had been full of fighting and unimaginable violence; none of it compared to the past ten minutes.

A few yards to his left, an officer rose and yelled, "Second Wisconsin, forward". Henry didn't think there was anyone left to charge except Arch and himself. But he could see more men with rifles coming out of the corn. With a shout the Iron Brigade rushed forward, heading for the Rebel line. Henry could just see, off in the distance down the Hagerstown Pike, a small white building. He didn't know it then, but this was the Dunker Church; it would become a fixture on the Antietam battlefield. Henry focused his attention on the enemy ahead; he carried a loaded rifle and paused once on the run to fire. He was pleased when he saw a Confederate officer drop his sword and clutch his chest as he fell. Now Henry was at an open rail fence bordering the road. Across the road, perhaps twenty feet away, was another fence with the enemy behind it. The men of the Second took what little cover the fence offered and let loose a volley at the Rebs. As the smoke cleared, Henry could see them running back toward a woods further on; except for those who lay dead and dying.

Further back up the road General Gibbon had ordered Battery B to move forward in support of the attack. The guns were placed in a rather open area but were giving the Confederates a hot time of it. Their shells were landing between the road and the woods just ahead of the brigade's position. The battery commander and his men were firing the guns as fast as they could, but Rebel bullets were beginning to take out men and horses.

At the fence Henry could see more Rebels forming in the woods, getting ready to attack. There were an awful lot of them and the Iron Brigade seemed too few to hold them back. Arch and Henry, side by side, continued to load and fire though it was difficult to see a target clearly through the dense smoke hanging in the still air. A breeze cleared the air just long enough for Henry to pick out a Rebel sergeant, stripes clearly visible along with his long gray beard. The southerner fired first and the bullet smacked into the fence rail next to Henry's head, sending splinters of wood into the side of his face. He fired just as the pain took hold; Henry watched as the sergeant's faced registered its own shock. The man grabbed his neck and Henry could actually see the blood pumping from between his fingers. Then he heard the order to fall back and protect the guns of Battery B; the Rebels were swinging around that way in an effort to capture the artillery.

Along the line, the men left what little shelter they had gained at the fence and headed back towards the battery. Now they were taking fire from behind and from their left as they moved along the road and back through the corn. Henry was having a hard time of it; between the pain in his face and all the bodies lying in the field, he tripped several times but never actually fell down. Arch was right there, giving him a hand when he needed it. He saw that his uncle's face was smeared black and gray from the powder and smoke and wondered what he looked like himself; probably worse, he thought. They arrived at the battery's position moments before the Confederate attack, taking position and turning toward the gray tide.

Henry kept telling himself, "Forget the face, fire and load". He was thankful that this fight had not become a hand to hand struggle; the only one of those he'd been in had cost him part of his nose. It was getting hard to ram the bullet down the barrel of his musket as the burnt powder built up inside it; he had nearly emptied all forty rounds he'd started with. Load and fire, load and fire. The Rebels came to within twenty feet of the cannon but didn't get any closer. The artillerymen, with their red trimmed uniforms, stood their ground and fired *double-shotted canister* into the very faces of the enemy. Dozens of men in gray disappeared as the small, round iron balls tore into them. It was like shooting quail or doves with a shotgun from a couple of feet away. Above the smoke, Henry saw the familiar red mist and body parts, arms and legs and heads and pieces of rifles and canteens flying about.

It was over; the Rebels ended their attempt at taking the battery and the battle seemed to be moving away, past the corn field down toward the little white building. Arch sat Henry down in what used to be an orchard near a small garden. "Lad, this will sting a bit," Arch said as he began to pull at the splinters in Henry's face. Another man came up and handed a small flask to Henry. "I know you're in need of some of this; might help a little," was all he said. Henry took a swallow and his throat burned at the taste, but a warmth followed and the pain slowly subsided. Arch worked at his face for several minutes, then poured some water from his canteen on a rag and washed the blood off. "Looks to be alright now, though your mother might hesitate giving you a kiss on that cheek for awhile." Arch sighed, the sigh of relief that a terrible thing was now over. Henry sat with the warm glow inside that matched the rising sun, climbing higher in the morning sky.

Lieutenant Winegar, just promoted from Sergeant Major a couple of weeks earlier, came over to check on Arch and Henry. Arch, puffing on his pipe, asked the Lieutenant how long they'd been in the fight. Pulling out a watch, Winegar said it looked like all of thirty minutes. "Sort of funny how you can live a whole lifetime in such a short while," was all Arch could reply. Henry added, "Seems like a lifetime of lifetimes these past three weeks."

That night Arch and Henry slept, or tried to, on the battlefield amid the horrors of the day's fight. All around them they could hear the moans and cries of the wounded; the lanterns of soldiers looking for comrades shown like hundreds of fireflies. An unofficial truce was observed by both sides as they worked together gathering the wounded they could find. However, not all the units still facing each other were so accommodating.

Every so often a shot would ring out in the distance; neither side seemed inclined to leave. Halfway through the night Henry got up and went over to a small fire near a farm house; there he met a half dozen other soldiers from both armies sharing coffee and some biscuits. He spoke with a young man from Virginia, not much older than himself. The Rebel was from a regiment in the Stonewall Brigade, their opponents from the fight at Brawner Farm.

"Y'all sure stood tall against us a couple weeks back. I knowed you're from the Black Hats cause of your long coat. I lost a brother and cousin in that fight, another brother today....don't know if I hanker on going back or just quittin' this here fight." The man said his name was Luke and he'd signed up to go to war in May of 1861. Henry took to him right away, they had much in common. "So why did you want to fight?" Henry asked Luke. "What did the North do to make you want to kill us?"

"Whall, it weren't what you did so much as the things I heard y'all were fixin' to do. Ya know, coloreds is sort of part of us in Virginia. Without them we'd not have enough folks to do all we got to get done. My pa said his ground ain't good for nothing but growing tobaccy and it takes too many hands to bring in the crop. Shoot, we only had three bucks ourselves, but if y'all had taken them away, we'd of starved or something. Folks were talking about Lincoln and his Republicans letting the abolitionists come down and takin' all the niggers back to Africa, or getting them to rise up and kill us all. I guess it was that what made me join up. Anyway, ain't no fun in it no more, just killing and watching friends and kin die. I'm thinking of sitting out the rest of it; I'm just not sure what my pa would do if'n he found out. Hey, what happened to your face anyway? You look a fright."

"Oh, it'll be alright; a ball hit the fence post I was kneeling behind. Could have been worse with no post at all. Hurts a lot, though; I guess I understand about other's talking you into signing on. It was kind of like that with me, back up in Wisconsin. I joined up in '61, in May, just like you. We heard that the South wanted a war and the Union was breaking up. We just couldn't stand for that....." Henry thought about that for a bit. Luke seemed like the sort he'd be friends with back home. He thought of Marcus; somehow he seemed to feel like his best friend was lost, never to be found. He got real sad at the thought, wondered what would happen if he just walked away tonight and kept walking until he got back to his home.....

The whole next day was one of waiting, kind of like a card game. Henry had never learned how to play but he'd watched Arch and the others. They would hold those cards and not smile, or blink or anything; just wait until someone else moved. Both armies did that now, neither General Lee nor General McClellan were going to attack or retreat. It seemed strange to the men of the Second Wisconsin that there was no more fighting; they liked the relative quiet, but they heard that almost half of their army was not even in the fight yesterday. Henry had heard from Luke and the other Rebels at the fire that Lee had used every soldier he had. The fighting had lasted all day and it seemed like the Federals had nearly broken through several times. Henry heard of General Burnside's attack at a bridge several miles to the south and of the horror of a sunken road some were calling Bloody Lane; how the Irish Brigade had almost been completely destroyed by the Rebels in the natural trench. Then two other Union brigades had moved up and caught the Rebs in a cross fire. One man Arch was talking with said the bodies in that road were five and six deep after the fighting died down.

Henry was able to go to a hospital that afternoon so he could get his face looked at. An orderly there was able to take some more splinters out but said there wasn't much else he could do. Henry was told to wash it with clean water; he had no idea where he could find any of that.

The creeks were running pink with blood and the well at the farm had dried up from so many soldiers needing water. That evening the men of his company were given rations of coffee and a steer to butcher and cook. It was too much meat for the fifteen that were still around so they invited some men from another company to share the beef and got some hardtack and apples to eat as well. The group found a gully to build a fire to cook over without drawing attention to themselves and had the best meal Henry and Arch could remember in a long while. Both of them slept well that night after talking about home; Arch reminded Henry of his duty to stay and not desert. Henry told his uncle he wasn't serious about leaving, but really missed home right now.

Chapter 13

Fall 1862

In the days following the battle along Antietam Creek the men of Company H were kept busy finding and burying the dead. Lee's army had retreated back into Virginia and McClellan was making no attempt at following. The second day of their work, just as they were finishing with the Union casualties and had started with the Confederates along the Hagerstown Pike, a wagon pulled up and two men got down and approached the burial detail. They said they were photographers and worked for a man in New York by the name of Matthew Brady. Arch did not recognize the name and the men seemed surprised; they explained that Mr Brady owned the most well known studio for portraits in the country and now wanted them to take images of the dead from the great battle. Henry went and explained to a Lieutenant in charge of the burial party and brought back his permission for the men to go to work.

After watching the men setting up their equipment, taking the images and working to develop the pictures, Arch frowned and said to the other soldiers standing nearby, "The darn fools are wasting half a day for what? Portraits of dead men that won't even care; this sort of thing will stink in the noses of the public as bad as the air here stinks in mine. No one will even know who they were or where they were from. You can have portrait studios and famous photographers. I don't think this thing will ever catch on." With that, he hoisted a shovel back on his shoulder and began digging a new ditch to put the dead men in when the photographers were done. Henry and the others pitched in as well and soon the unknown Rebels along the Pike were in a new home, three feet under ground.

The next day Henry's face was hurting and was red and swollen around the largest of the splinter wounds. Arch went with him to the division hospital, about one quarter mile away. As they neared the place, which used to be a farmyard and small orchard, they could hear the moaning and the smell was nearly as bad as the dead men they had buried. They entered an area where shelter halves were strung between bushes in an attempt to keep the hot sun off the wounded. Men were crying for water; Arch could only see one orderly and two women caring for more than a hundred wounded. Near the only shed in sight, what was a small hen coop, they saw a pile of arms and legs that had been removed by the surgeons. Henry's eyes were wide open and white with fear; he told Arch they had to leave and get back to their own area. The sights, sounds and smell of the place were more than the young man could endure. "I'd rather have my face fall off than spend one hour in this place", he was telling Arch as they left. "I don't care what happens, I will not go to a hospital like this one; I think Marcus did and he's just disappeared now." Arch did not have anything to say that would change how Henry felt; deep inside, he agreed with his nephew.

Arch decided to nurse Henry's face himself; by carefully washing the wounds with clean water and dressing them with some salve an Ojibway half-breed from another company gave him, the cuts and scratches improved within a few days. The deeper wounds took a full week to get better but in the end the scars were not too bad, though there were plenty of them on the left side of Henry's face. When he looked at his reflection in a mirror a couple of weeks later, Henry mused that none of the girls in Dekorra would go on a picnic with him now. "And you think they would have before?" was the answer he got from Arch and the others.

The news that President Lincoln had issued a proclamation that was to free the slaves at the beginning of the new year was not altogether well received by the northern troops. Though most of the Wisconsin men approved of the President and his intentions, many men in the 19th Indiana, especially those from the southern part of that state, did not agree. They said they had joined to preserve the Union and not to free any slaves. "Let the south keep their slaves and come back into our country" was what many of them believed.

The Iron Brigade was formed up by regiments to meet and greet their newest addition. As promised by General McClellan, another western regiment was added to their numbers; the recently formed 24th Michigan Volunteers, fresh from Detroit. Their clean, crisp uniforms and blue caps were a distinct contrast to the shabby, worn coats and dirty, crumpled hats of the veterans. When they were introduced, no one cheered. The new recruits would have to prove themselves to the grizzled, tanned and lean men that had earned the brigade its name. Soon another change would occur that would rankle them; word came down that General Gibbon was being given command of the Division and the senior Colonel, by date of rank, would be Colonel Morrow. He was the commander of the 24th Michigan and had not yet been in a single fight.

President Lincoln came to the camp to review the Iron Brigade and to show his personal appreciation for the fighting they had done over the past two months. The regiments marched past him with coats brushed clean and brass shined and leather blackened, looking as solid as their name implied. The President took time to walk among the men after the parade, as he often did, greeting them as individuals with kind words and a friendly handshake. As he stood chatting with Arch; both men towering above the others, Lincoln in his tall stovepipe hat and Arch in his equally tall Hardee, a short and burly Irish sergeant attempted to squeeze between them. The man seemed to barely reach to their belt buckles as he muttered in his thick brogue, "Begorra, I be splittin' the rails meself". It was a moment that broke the ice; the men of the brigade cheered their commander in chief until they were hoarse. It was as though the built up tension of weeks of hard marching and fierce combat had dissolved in that instant and they could relax, let the tightness they all felt just disappear.

"I'm glad to be on the move again. I know it's important that those Michigan boys learn how to fight with us and their numbers will definitely help in the days ahead, but the war won't get won if we don't go after the Rebs." Henry was his old, talkative self and Arch was glad for it. The spirits of all the men in the brigade had improved with the rest and refit they got after Antietam. They had read in the Washington papers of the nation's impatience with General McClellan's insistence that the army not move until it was ready to fight again. "He's got the slows", was one quote of Lincoln himself about the Army of the Potomac's commander. Now they were on the roads leading into Virginia and there was still enough autumn left for another campaign.

The Iron Brigade crossed the Potomac into Virginia and halted. The men would have to get used to the angry stares of the people they saw; there was no more of the happy, grateful faces they had seen in Maryland. They camped at a town called Warrenton in an area they had marched past several times before. It was strange to find out that their temporary brigade commander, Colonel Morrow, had been born in this town and his mother was actually buried in the cemetery less than a mile from their camp. It looked like they would be settling in awhile; orders were issued for no foraging and to leave the fences alone. Firewood was to be cut from the wooded areas nearby, no more of the "top rail only" destruction they enjoyed the past spring.

"This does not bode well for us, I'm afraid. Lieutenant Winegar just told me McClellan has been relieved and General Burnside is our new army commander. It looks like Secretary Stanton and the President have had enough of Little Mac's caution. I'm sure it means we'll be having that fight you've been looking forward to lad." Arch had just returned with their rations for the day; two crackers each, some salt pork and a bit of coffee. The army had been plagued with an inability to feed the men since they moved out of Maryland. Each day they were getting less and less to eat and no one knew why. It was being called the Warrenton Famine now and had been going on for nearly a week. Some figured the leaders in Washington were using the lack of food as a way to get the army to move on. Henry only knew his stomach was grumbling more and louder than the soldiers in the camp. "Uncle Arch, I'm not really looking forward to another fight, I just think we need to win the war as quick as we can and it seems like beating Lee's army is the way to do it. We can keep marching and stopping forever without killing a single one of them; I don't want to live here in Virginia any longer than I have to."

The army moved two days later and made good time on the dry roads, the march took them down to a place called Falmouth, just across the Rappahannock River from Fredericksburg. There were few, if any, Rebels on the other side and it looked like the town would be gained quickly and without casualties; until the army stopped again. Though the river could be forded easily in several places, General Burnside decided to wait for the pontoon bridge supplies to arrive from the rear of the army column. This wait allowed the Confederates under General Lee to arrive and occupy the town of Fredericksburg. More importantly, the high ground behind the town was now heavily fortified by the Rebels. The Iron Brigade was shifted downriver to the Federal left and crossed the river on December 11th at the head of General Doubleday's division. They also had a new permanent brigade commander, General Solomon Meredith, who had commanded the 19th Indiana Volunteers.

Chapter 14

Fredericksburg

"Uncle, I think it's great that you've made corporal. I can still talk to you, can't I?" Henry was proud of Arch's new promotion and the stripes on his blouse looked grand.

"Listen, lad; you can speak, but do it with the proper respect." Arch's grin was nearly as wide as his new stripes which wrapped halfway around his upper arms. "Of course, when there are only 11 of us left in the company, about the only private left is yourself. I think you had better look to that flaw in your character Henry."

The two were sitting at a very small fire, well shielded to not give away their position to the enemy. The coffee was just beginning to boil and the smell made Henry's mouth water. They had marched along the river to the far left end of the Federal line and the Rebels were close by, perhaps only 100 yards. Before dark, skirmishers had reported that General Jeb Stuart's cavalry and some horse artillery were blocking the road along the river. The brigade's orders were to hold this position and prepare for an attack up the hills that rose away from the water. Even in the dim starlight the outline of those hills could be seen; a few small fires, like their own, flickered along the crest of the hills. They were almost two miles from the town of Fredericksburg but they could see the glow of the fires burning in the town. The other corps of the Union army had taken the town earlier in the day;

they had used pontoons as boats to ferry troops across the river to drive out the Rebel sharpshooters that had been killing the engineers trying to build the bridges for the rest of the army to cross. Now the town was theirs and many northern troops were looting and burning houses. It made Henry and Arch, and many others, angry that this was allowed to happen. "No point in giving the enemy more to be mad about" was how one sergeant had put it when they heard some of the stories. "I'm sure Johnny Reb will give us a warm enough welcome when we march up to his guns on those hills in the morning."

After their coffee and a cracker, Henry and Arch curled up under their blankets, sharing them to keep warm on this cold December night. The brigade had not brought their tents across the river and as the temperature dropped, frost formed on the sleeping bodies by morning. They knew they had not come to stay; the sixty rounds each man carried in their pouch and pockets reminded them of the serious work ahead. No extra clothing, no packs; just weapons, ammunition, water and three days' rations. It all added up to a fight.

When the two woke the next morning, the other divisions of the First Corps were already forming up on the plain in front of the hills. Doubleday's division, including the Iron Brigade was to protect the left flank from Stuart's horsemen and his artillery, the same pesky guns they had faced at Brawner Farm in their first real fight. But they had Battery B with them, and had shown them what for then; maybe they'd do it again.

The shells were coming closer as the Rebel gunners got the range. Company H, along with two others, were assigned to protect the guns of the battery. The rest of the Second Wisconsin was out ahead with the brigade clearing the southern infantry from the woods in their front. The Union gunners were firing in a quick rhythm that always amazed Henry. He marveled as each man at a gun performed his job with precision and speed. The guns barked nearly as fast as he could fire his own musket. With each cannon firing twice a minute, the four guns put a shell toward the enemy every 8 or so seconds. Many of the men working them were from the infantry regiments; they had been recruited months back to take the places of men killed at Second Bull Run and Antietam.

A Confederate solid shot bounced ahead of them and Arch and Henry watched as it took off the leg of an artilleryman and cut another in half before it bounded past. Henry jumped up and, handing his musket to Arch, ran to the gun to replace one of the two. He had watched often enough to take the place of the one whose job had been to wheel the gun back forward after it fired and rolled back. It was fast paced, hard work but Henry was enjoying it; he had been working with the gun crew about 15 minutes when the enemy shell went off to his left. The blast lifted him off the ground and threw him against the hot barrel of the cannon. Henry felt the heat and heard the sizzling of his own skin before he fell to the ground. Everything went black...

Lieutenant Winegar directed Arch to take Henry to the regimental surgeon back across the river. With the help of another soldier, Arch was able to get him safely there. Behind him the First Corps was beginning to fall back from the attack they had made against Stonewall Jackson's troops on the hill. Stuart's cavalry and horse artillery had been driven back by the Iron Brigade but they, too, were now ordered to fall back to their original position.

Surgeon Ward was already beginning to treat the wounded coming in from the battle. He had Arch place Henry on a door that served as a table in one of the tents. Henry was conscious now and the pain on the right side of his face was horrible. Dr. Ward was busy cleaning the burns as best he could, removing dirt and grass. Henry's face was burned from his right temple to his chin and his right eye was already swollen shut. He told the doctor he could not open it but could "roll his eye" and feel it move. After cleaning the burns, Dr. Ward spoke with Arch outside the tent. "Private McCollum is a lucky one; I don't think the eye is permanently damaged, though time will tell more. The burns are pretty bad and I'm sure they will scar up quite a bit. Might have a hard time smiling and probably won't wink with the right eye. He has no broken bones or other injuries I can see. Let him rest here for awhile and he can go back after we put a fresh dressing on his face. I'll put him in for a furlough to go back to Wisconsin; I know his father and he has more experience in treating burns than I do. A month or so at home will help in other ways as well, I'm sure."

Chapter 15

Winter 1862

Henry's convalescent trip back to Dekorra began two days later with a wagon ride to the railroad connection outside Washington. Arch was allowed to accompany him to the train depot; their farewell was emotional in a way family caught in a war can understand. No tears, just heart felt expressions of hope that they would see each other again. Arch sent along his earnings for the past several months for Henry to give to his father for safekeeping, along with a list of items Arch wanted him to bring back when he returned. "You know there won't be any fighting before I get back; the walloping Lee gave us at Fredericksburg will make our generals lay low awhile. Anyway, you're a corporal with big responsibilities, like not getting yourself shot." Henry was trying to put the grown up look on the half of his face that was visible.

"Lad, be alert and careful on the train. You've three days to Madison and there are all kinds of ruffians and scoundrels about these days. Give your mother a hug from me and your father a good handshake. Say hello to the folks I know and be sure to bring back those things on the list I gave you. We'll both be needing much of that before we're done with this war. I best be getting back, your train will be leaving in a few minutes anyhow. You be sure to come back." With that, Arch turned and strode away, without looking back once. Henry was instantly alone and lonely.

A man showed Henry where to put his gear and he sat down in his seat. The car he was in was nearly empty; this first run was a short one to Baltimore. He was supposed to have a few hours there before his train to Chicago would board and leave. He planned on eating some of whatever Baltimore had to offer and then sleep, maybe if he was lucky, all the way to Illinois. The seat he was on was about the most comfortable thing he'd been on since he could remember. A couple of the officers in the regiment went and bought him actual tickets for the trip home so he wouldn't have to use a bench like most soldiers traveled on. He noticed a cavalry officer in the car with his right sleeve pinned up on his shoulder, evidence of having lost the arm. Another officer, this one was in the artillery, boarded with help and sat down; Henry saw he had one wooden foot and no other leg below the knee. Henry suddenly felt very humble and thankful that his injury was only burns on his face.

A man, his wife and two children boarded the car next. The man and wife sat together and the children each took a seat to themselves. The son, nearly Henry's age, came over and sat across the aisle. "Howdy, soldier, what happened to you? Did you lose the eye under that dressing as well as your nose?"

Henry managed a bit of a smile and said, "Small price to pay for what I did to the Reb that took my nose. I can use my right eye, just burned around it so I have to keep it covered, too. What's your name lad?"

"My name is Robert; my father is a business owner in Chicago and we've been in Washington, meeting the President. I don't suppose you've ever seen him, have you?" The boy was not boastful, just honestly curious.

"As a fact, I have. Mr. Lincoln reviewed our brigade a couple months back in Maryland, just after Antietam. I got to shake his hand." Henry would always remember that moment, along with the Irish sergeant's remark that day.

"Father, Mother, come meet this soldier; he was at Antietam!" The boy was practically dragging his father over to meet Henry and was very excited to be able to introduce his parents to a real soldier.

Robert's father, Richard Patterson, shook Henry's hand and thanked him for helping to defend the Union. His wife, Ellie, greeted Henry kindly and asked where he was traveling to. Mr. Patterson was interested to hear more from an Iron Brigade member; he had read quite a bit in the Chicago papers about the westerners. The short ride to Baltimore went by quickly and soon Henry had been invited to dinner with the Pattersons. Mrs. Patterson was quite surprised to find out that Henry was only seventeen; "Why, Robert is nearly sixteen and look at you. You've been fighting in the army nearly two years!!! Your mother must be worried half to death about you. I know I would be."

Henry explained how he, Marcus and Uncle Arch had all joined up together to help each other. Now Arch was back in Virginia and no one knew anything about what had happened to Marcus since the Brawner Farm fight. Henry was not looking forward to meeting Marcus' family in a few days; he knew he'd have to tell them their son had simply disappeared.

"Well", said Mrs. Patterson, "At least you'll be home for Christmas. What a wonderful gift that will be for your parents."

The Pattersons knew of a restaurant in Baltimore that served very good food. Mr. Patterson insisted on paying for Henry's dinner; he said "It is a small thing compared to the price you've already paid to help secure freedom for others." When they boarded the next train bound for Chicago, Henry tried his hardest to fulfill the promise he'd made to himself; he slept for hours and hours while the train traveled and stopped for wood, water and to transfer other passengers. When he woke up, Robert explained that they had already crossed Pennsylvania and were well into Ohio. Henry felt better; the pain was less and his body rested.

The rest of the trip was spent in pleasant conversation with the Pattersons and with Henry dozing off for long 'naps', usually after they had eaten. When the train reached Chicago, Richard Patterson asked Henry if he would care to stay a day or so to see the city before continuing on to Madison. Henry politely declined the invitation; he wanted to get home as soon as he could. Mr. Patterson certainly understood this, and said Henry would be welcome to visit them on his way back to the front after his convalescence. The family departed for their home and Henry was left alone with a few hours to spend in the station. He purchased his ticket to Madison and found the telegraph office around the corner. He paid for a telegram to be sent to his father's office in Dekorra and was a bit surprised that it cost the same as three days' pay for him, nearly a whole dollar. He did want his parents to know he had reached Chicago and would arrive in Madison in the morning.

The next day, shortly before noon, the train pulled in to the Wisconsin capital. No one was at the station to greet him so he started on the road to Dekorra. Being as it was only 30 or so miles, he figured it was much more pleasant than a march in hot Virginia. The weather was much cooler, but there was no snow on the ground and the sky was a bright blue, no clouds to be seen. Twice along the way, farmers offered him a ride in their wagon and Henry figured he'd only hiked about half the distance to home. He knew better than to surprise his mother, especially with his face all bandaged up, so he walked into his father's office. Henry knew he would be in as it was before supper time and the light was on in the office window.

Chapter 16

Christmas 1862

"Good afternoon, Father." Henry had opened the door softly, like someone trying to sneak out in the middle of the night. His father, James, was taken completely by surprise.

"Henry!! What on earth are you doing home? My God, son, what's happened to you? Come over here under the light; you need a clean bandage on that face after I take a look at you. No need to cause your mother the same shock you just gave me. Land's sake, why didn't you write that you were coming home?"

"I did, Father. In fact I sent a telegram from Chicago yesterday that I'd be arriving. I was only granted my furlough the day before I was put on the train from Alexandria, Virginia. I didn't think the mail would arrive before I did; a telegram didn't either."

James removed the covering on the side of Henry's face, and his look said a lot. The burns were pretty severe and the best opportunity to treat them right had already passed. He was amazed, and very proud, that his son was able to even stand with the pain that must accompany a wound like this. Henry didn't utter a sound as his father worked at removing bits of burned flesh and dirt from the burn.

"This will leave a pretty good scar, son, but the eye seems fine and clear. I don't think you'll be growing much hair above that ear either. Good heavens, how did this happen? It looks like someone hit you with a hot pipe or something."

"Actually, sir, I hit it. I was thrown against a cannon barrel when a Rebel shell went off near me. We were in the middle of a fight and I only remember hitting something really hot....then Uncle Arch was over me and helping me off the field. The rest happened pretty fast and here I am. I think it was a week ago today, I'm not really even sure what day today is."

"Son, it's the solstice, December 21st. Christmas is a few days away; Mother will be glad to know you and Arch are safe. She'll be thrilled that you're here for awhile. How long can you stay to heal up?"

"I'm supposed to be back with the regiment on the 20th of January. We were camped a bit south of Alexandria, not far from the rail head. I suppose that's where I'll find them when I go back. But that's not for weeks and right now I could use something to eat. Do you suppose Mother has enough for three?"

"If not, I know I'll go hungry just to see you get enough." James thumped his son on the back and they went out into the early darkness of a December night.

"Marie, there's someone outside wanting a bite to eat. Can we invite him in for supper with us?" James was speaking softly to Marie while she was putting the final touches to their meal. As she turned to remind him that she only cooked for two now, she saw the bandaged face of her son in the doorway.

"Henry!!!! Good Lord, are you alright? What happened to you? Is Arch with you? Sit down; for heaven's sake, James, you might have told me! What an entrance you make, nearly sneaking in like this." Marie feigned irritation, but was feeling light as a feather inside as she hugged and kissed her son. Her mother's eyes looked right past the nose and scars on the face to see her boy.

After the meal was done, Marie said there was practically no need to wash the dishes as it appeared Henry had licked them clean. "In fact, Mother, we almost never wash anything. Water is often hard to come by and what we get we drink. A bit of sand rubbed on a plate will clean it fine as well. Now, come sit down and tell me what has been happening in this part of the country since I left. Telling others of what I've been through is tiresome and I need to hear of more happy things."

Christmas in the McCollum house was a quiet affair. Under different circumstances James and Marie would have invited the entire town of Dekorra to a reception for Henry. He had insisted that they ask Marcus' family to join them for a feast of wild turkey, fish, venison and a bear roast that Mr Dufrense provided. The atmosphere was somewhat sober with the absence of Henry's best friend, but with that many children in the house, it wasn't entirely quiet.

"So you haven't been able to learn anything of Marcus or where he may be?" Mrs Defrense wore a weary expression on her face. He was the oldest of their seven children and his hard work would be sorely missed in helping the family.

"No, ma'am; not a thing. We know he was out with the skirmishers in front of the regiment at Brawner's Farm. We heard the next day that someone thought they had seen him wounded and being carried from the field. But none of the surgeons remembered him or anything. Uncle Arch and I even hoped he had been captured, but there should have been word of that by now. Things got real busy right after that fight, what with Second Manassas, South Mountain and Antietam all following in the next couple of weeks. I'm terribly sorry I can't bring better news about Marcus. We all miss him, along with the others that are missing. There aren't more than 20 of the original 100 of the company left, and that was before this latest battle at Fredericksburg." Henry was hurting now; his face and his heart.

James McCollum could not get to sleep that night. He kept seeing faceless boys on tables with tired surgeons working on them, ready to collapse from exhaustion. He had read the papers, had heard the calls for more doctors for the army. Fighting in this modern war was terrible beyond anything experienced before. This last battle at Fredericksburg had cost the Union more than 12,000 casualties while the Confederates had lost nearly 5,000. It seemed the entire country would be bled dry by this awful conflict. He determined what he would do; he felt it his duty as a doctor to go and help, to volunteer in a new Wisconsin regiment advertising for a surgeon. His decision made, James fell fast asleep.

Chapter 17

New Year 1863

The family was invited to a special reception for New Year's Day. Five other soldiers were home in Dekorra, recuperating like Henry. It was as festive as could be expected; the six soldiers were heaped with praise and two German families brought three kegs from the Rodermund brewery in Madison. People in the area said John Rodermund's Buck Beer was the best in the state. A couple from near Arch's farm came and provided music on a fiddle and a flute. Two of the wounded each tapped their one foot; after the first steins of beer were gone, they compared shoe sizes and determined they could share one pair between them. Practically everyone Henry knew was at the party; all but the MacDonald family. They were in Milwaukee for a week visiting relatives and would not return for a couple more days. Susan MacDonald was the one person Henry really wanted to see again. They had been friends in school before the war and some said she was the prettiest girl in town now. As the reception came to a close, final toasts were given to the Union, President Lincoln and victory. The six soldiers were honored one more time and people started heading home.

It was a brisk mile walk for the McCollums. A breeze had come up from the north and snow was lightly drifting down from the gray sky. The three of them walked arm in arm; Marie in the center, happy to be with her two men. James was deep in thought and Henry was a bit wobbly from the beer. James stoked the stove when they got home; the warmth and the soft chair combined with the brew to put Henry asleep quickly. Marie and James sat close together and watched their son. James reminded Marie of how Henry could never sleep anywhere but his own bed when he was much younger. "I imagine he could drop off just about anywhere now", he said. Marie sighed and answered, "Yes, dear, but it's grand to have him right here, right now. I'm glad Arch is safe, too; this war has gone on longer than anyone would have believed. When will it end? The south seems to keep winning even though we are so much stronger. The first night Henry was home I prayed the fighting would end before he has to return. Now it's only two more weeks."

"Dear, there's something else we need to talk about. I have not had a moment's peace since he got home. All I can think about are the hundreds, maybe thousands, of young men like Henry... even my own brother, that don't have surgeons to care for them. The army is woefully short of qualified people. Men are dying because there are not enough to care for them after these large battles, and the battles don't seem to be getting smaller. Last night I decided it's time for me to volunteer as well. I know you'll be fine; we can have you stay with your sister in Kenosha, on the lake. It's much closer to our families in Chicago as well."

Marie moved closer, wrapping her arms around her husband, her head on his shoulder. "I knew this was coming, I've sensed it for days now. You would have gone with Henry and Arch if you could have. I suppose you'll be going to Madison with Henry on his way back? Might I go then as well, so I can say goodbye to you both together?" She was starting to sob, just a bit, when the last words were spoken.

They all awoke to a sunny, cold morning with frost on the windows and hoar frost coating the trees and bushes; everything looked like white lace. James had expected more resistance from Marie about his decision to join the army. He wasn't at all prepared for what Henry had to say; he was glad, though, that Henry chose to speak when Marie was not there.

"Father, please don't do this. I've seen more terrible things than a person should have to. I've had men die beside me with their blood and brains spattering my face and uniform. Terrible wounds, bodies blown to pieces in front of me. You do not want to do this. It would not be fair to mother to have both of us gone. I'm home now, safe in this house; but I know I'll go back and I don't think I'll ever see home again."

James let him have his say. "Son, I've given this much thought. I have a duty as well as you. You'll go back to answer that call; well, I have a call as well. There's a new regiment forming in Madison, the 23rd Wisconsin. They need a surgeon. I don't even know if I'll be going east or down to Tennessee. That's where nearly all of the western troops are fighting now. Mother will be well with her sister and close to the rest of the family. When the war is over, we will all, even Arch, have the biggest celebration ever. I plan on leaving with you, mother as well. There's much to do and arrange if we're to go in two weeks. I'll be needing your help with this."

Chapter 18

January 1863

Wisconsin

A few days following the New Year reception Henry's bandages were removed. From just below his right eye to the corner of his mouth and up to above the right ear was a large scab. Henry could see out of the eye but the brightness bothered him; his father explained that the sensitivity to light should pass in just a few hours. He also instructed his son to keep salve on the scab and to not pick or scratch at it. James was sure it would heal alright but there would definitely be scarring. Henry was just glad to be rid of the bandage and to have both eyes working.

He walked out of his father's office and bumped into a lovely young woman. Her expression when she saw his face caused Henry to turn his head and hurry away. He knew she hadn't recognized him and the look in her eyes twisted his gut and made his heart ache. This was not how he wanted to meet Susan MacDonald again.

Henry hurried to the house and bolted for his room. He took one look in the mirror at the washstand and saw, not a boy but a disfigured ogre with a torn nose, scarred and burned face and eyes full of misery. Henry did not come out of his room for the rest of the day. He grunted that he was not hungry when his mother called him down for the noon meal. At supper his father came up and opened the door; Henry was face down on his bed. "She saw me as the monster I've become, father. I was fooling myself into believing it would be alright, that I would look fairly normal. But I don't; I look like a ghoul. Now I know I won't be coming back to Dekorra, or Wisconsin, at all. When I return to the army, all that awaits me is my grave."

His father's heart was breaking. "I'll bring you up a bit of supper. Try to get some rest and not think about this further tonight. You've had a shock, maybe greater than any while fighting. We'll talk in the morning." James went back downstairs and had Marie fix a plate. He took a sedative and mixed it in Henry's food to help him sleep. Then he told his wife they would be going out for a short visit across town and that Henry would be sleeping soon.

Cedric MacDonald answered the door; he was surprised to find the McCollum's outside. "Come in, come in. It's not a night to be standing out in this cold, now is it? What would be bringing you to this house anyway, Doctor?"

"Good evening, Cedric. Marie and I need to speak with you and your daughter for a moment, if you please. It would be good if your wife joined us as well. There is a situation with Henry and..."

"I'd heard the boy was home. We just arrived in town today ourselves; we've been with family. How is the lad? And what news do you have of your brother, Arch? We read of Fredericksburg while we were away; frightful, dreadful slaughter. I prayed that neither Henry nor Arch were killed." MacDonald was leading the way through the house to the rear parlor, where the lights were on and the fire sharing its warmth. Harriet was just finishing a letter to her family; she put down the quill and closed the inkwell.

"Doctor, Marie, this is a surprise. Come, sit down. I'll just put the kettle back on; tea will only take a minute. We just returned, you know." Marie went with her into the kitchen to help.

"Cedric, I hope your trip was safe and you found your family well. It can be a challenge to travel this time of year; you never know just when the weather will turn on you." James was not comfortable with small talk; he would rather get to the matter at hand. "And how is Susan? I imagine she's glad to be home again?"

"Actually, James, the damndest thing happened today. Susan went walking to find out what she's missed the past weeks and came home frightened like a little puppy. She said a man nearly bowled her over near your office without so much as a 'Sorry, miss'. According to her, you'd think it was the devil himself. She says he's all cut up and bloody in the face. Do you know anything about this, James, was this man a patient of yours?"

"It was Henry. He arrived a couple of weeks ago; he was wounded at Fredericksburg. The army sent him home to heal and we had no word he was coming. He's been gone more than a year, nearly two, and it's taken a toll on him, that's for sure. He's had three wounds; now he's sure that he looks horrible and deserves a soldier's death when he goes back. That's in another two weeks."

The rest of the visit was longer than expected; spent in the four parents talking over the encounter between Susan and Henry, which led to discussions about the war, the country and Dekorra. James did not speak of his decision to join the army. He felt it best to approach the two other doctors closest to the town first; to let them know that their practices would soon expand. He planned to do this very soon.

Over the next few days, Henry's outlook brightened with the arrival of the "January thaw", a period of slightly warmer weather that often comes in mid-month and is so welcome by those living in the extreme northern states. He realized that he had best put on a few pounds of weight before he returned to the brigade. The way he figured it, being fat when he returned would show Arch and the others that he had enjoyed himself at home. He still carried the hurt deep inside that his looks could frighten someone, but part of him was hoping it would work as well on the Rebels. He could hear Corporal Moore, from the town of Lodi, say "Yep, thar's nuthin' quite like givin' that other guy a right good scare, just afore you blow his head off." Henry chuckled to himself, felt a little piece of him inside missing "the boys". He knew he'd feel even better when he was back with those that knew just how he felt. Civilians, especially family, just didn't.... well, they hadn't "seen the elephant"; they could read about the war, but until those *minie balls* were buzzing by your head, you just couldn't understand.

That afternoon a letter was brought home by his father. It was from Susan MacDonald and apologized for her reaction the other day. She mentioned it would be nice for Henry to write now and then to her folks letting them know how he was. By this time Henry was able to accept the note and what he thought it didn't say; that he would pretty much be wasting his time thinking about Susan anymore. It made him sad for a moment, but the hardness he saw in so many other soldiers was growing in him. He was becoming less consumed with the thought of dying; he thought it just might do to actually live through this war and come home again. That would show them all that getting shot to pieces wouldn't stop Henry McCollum.

The next ten days were full of packing, making arrangements with Mr Dufrense to care for the house while they were away. Marie couldn't bear the thought of selling it right away so it was decided to close it up until summer. James hired a local farmer and his son to drive a wagon to Kenosha with the things Marie would need while living with her sister. Mr Dufrense drove them to Madison in a carriage. James and Marie saw Henry off on the Chicago train and, later that day, Marie took another to Milwaukee where her sister would meet her. Few words were spoken at the station; they had said their goodbyes on the ride down from Dekorra. James was alone now and went directly to Camp Randall to report as the surgeon for the 23rd Wisconsin Infantry.

"Henry... Henry McCollum, is that really you?" The voice caused Henry to look up; he was just beginning to doze in the warm sunshine coming in through the coach window. At first he didn't recognize the officer, a Captain, who was standing looking down at him. Henry blinked once or twice, cleared the gathering cobwebs of a nap, and jumped up.

"Mr Patterson, I mean... uhh, Captain Patterson? What a surprise, sir, to meet you again. The second time I'm on a train and I meet you....in a uniform?"

"You know Henry," Captain Patterson said as he sat next to Henry, "When I got back to our house I couldn't help thinking about you, just a year or so older than my own son, and your willingness to fight in this war. I almost felt ashamed that I hadn't felt the same when the fighting started. I finally figured that if I joined up, maybe my son won't have to when he's your age. So, here I am, brand new and going to serve as a quartermaster for General Wadsworth. I have to report to him in Virginia in a couple of days. Have you ever heard of him?"

"Yes, sir. General Wadsworth is my own division commander. The Iron Brigade is the Second Brigade in the First Division of the First Corps under General Reynolds." Noting the look of bewilderment on the Captain's face, Henry continued. "Sir, I can draw it out for you... here, my regiment, the Second Wisconsin is part of the Second Brigade; we're called the Iron Brigade and have four other regiments in it. I don't know just how many men we have now after so much fighting, maybe a couple of thousand. Anyway, there are, as I recall, two other brigades in Wadsworth's Division and a couple more divisions in the First Corps. It's how the army is made up; I'm sure they'll explain it all to you when you get there." Henry was dumbfounded that a grown man, an officer, didn't know how the army was organized.

"Oh, I'm sure they will. General Wadsworth is my wife's uncle and when I talked of joining up to fight, well, Mrs Patterson couldn't resist contacting her uncle and now I'm to be on his staff. It's all pretty sudden, but it will be safe and I feel I'm doing my part. I do hope to see you from time to time if we're to be in the same..... what did you call it, yes, the same division. You know, I've been a good businessman, I know how to own and run a milling operation, but the army is pretty confusing. I'm sure I'll catch on for the ride shortly."

"I'm sure you will, sir. If I get a chance, I'll try to look you up at division headquarters. I'll talk to my company officers, I'm sure it will be alright. Then you can meet my uncle Arch; he's a corporal now."

Captain Patterson was pleased. "Splendid, I'd enjoy meeting him. Will I have to salute him, or is a Captain higher ranking than a Corporal?"

"Sir, let me go over a few things with you while we travel. First, you start with a Private like me...."

Chapter 19

January 1863

Virginia

"Captain Patterson? I'm Lieutenant Adams, one of General Wadsworth's staff; if you'll follow me, sir, I'm to bring you to the General's tent." The young man in the uniform didn't look any older than Henry, though Henry had certainly aged a bit in the past year and a half.

Turning to Henry, Captain Patterson held out his hand. "Private McCullom, thank you for the help you've given me on the train." In a quieter voice he whispered, "If you want a job at Division headquarters, I'll see what can be done."

"Thank you, sir, but I'll be getting back to the regiment. I'm sure they can use another body there as well. I'm sure I'll see you again, sir."

Lieutenant Adams picked up the Captain's bags and was walking briskly down the station platform. The Captain turned to go with the parting words, "You keep your head down out there, Henry McCollum."

Henry picked up his own kit and headed off to find the Second Wisconsin. There was a small city of tents in the near distance and he figured it was a place to get information on where they were camped. "Just a stretch of the legs", Henry thought to himself as he started out. It ended up being a six mile hike before he found the Iron Brigade's area. Arch was sitting on a cracker box, blackening some of his leather when Henry strode up. "Well, well, what have we here? It looks almost like a soldier, walks almost like a soldier, but it doesn't smell like a soldier; not yet, anyway." He stood up and gave Henry a handshake and a hug. Henry sat down and started to tell Arch of his trip home and back while his uncle stirred the fire and set a pot of water to boiling for some coffee.

It was a good hour later that Henry finally got around to remembering the items he brought that Arch had wanted. Thread, needles, buttons, writing paper, pencils, a toothbrush and powder, new razor and strop, and other small but important things needed on the march. He took out the last item, carefully, and handed it to Arch. "I've guarded this all the way from Dekorra; tried to keep it as cool as I could." It was a sealed bottle of John Rodermund's Buck Beer, probably the first of its kind ever in Virginia.

"Oh, lad, I should be giving you stripes for this. Warm or cool, this is going to go down well." Arch opened the bottle and took a drink. "Ahhhh, life in the army was never better. Thank you, Henry. Welcome home."

Henry quickly settled in to the routine of camp life. Drilling, eating, cleaning uniforms and equipment, more drill and a little marching thrown in was the army recipe to prevent too much boredom in camp. It was winter in Virginia, too, and the brigade wasn't going too far until spring dried up the roads.

Chapter 20

February 1863

"Henry, you got three letters today. Let's see, one from your mother, one from your father, and one... it's from Dekorra but I can't make out the name." Arch puffed on his pipe while Henry read the letters to him. His mother had settled in with her sister in Kenosha and was worried about her "two boys in Virginia". She had only received one letter from Henry's father so far, it was posted from St Louis, Missouri. James had written while on his way to meet up with his regiment in Arkansas. He read the same information from his father's letter. He was busy learning the army's language and way of doing things as well while he was traveling. He did write that there were not many railroads, mostly river travel where he was going. The third letter was from the MacDonald family. Mrs MacDonald had written it and included a short note from Susan; Henry was surprised that she had actually done this. His heart lifted a bit but he was careful not to read too much into getting the letter. This letter he didn't share with Arch; he only said who it was from.

A few days later part of the Second was sent, along with two companies of the Sixth Wisconsin, on a foraging and scouting mission down the river from their camp. These forays were intended to keep the edge on their fighting abilities and to help instruct new officers. As it happened,

Captain Patterson was going along on this one. The expedition, numbering about 500 men, was divided into three groups. Company H, including Henry and Arch, were in a unit commanded by Major Mansfield of the Second. As they were searching a plantation they discovered a cache of more than 10,000 pounds of bacon. The plantation owner was immediately arrested on suspicion of smuggling food to the Rebels. Nearly 70 former slaves helped load the food onto wagons for the return trip back to camp. They then followed the soldiers north to freedom.

"Private McCollum, a fine day for a march isn't it?" Captain Patterson was riding beside the column and happened upon Henry and Arch.

"Yes, sir, it is that. Not too warm, good road, no Rebels. That does add up to a fine march. What did you think of this whole affair, sir?"

"Splendid, splendid. If this is what war is about, I'm only sorry I didn't join up earlier. I'm sure there's more to it though. My job now will be to get these new found stores distributed in the division. I'll be sure to get plenty sent to the Second. Would this happen to be your uncle you told me about?"

"Yes, sir, this is my Uncle Arch... er, Corporal Archibald McCollum that is."

"It's a pleasure to meet you, Corporal. Your nephew has been a wonderful instructor to me in the ways of this Army. Don't know how I would have made it through my first day without his coaching. Well, I'd best be on my way to securing all this plunder." With that he rode away.

"And that would be the officer you met on your way back here?" Arch asked Henry. "Seems like he's got a bit more to learn about soldiering. At least he's smart enough to get a horse to do his walking for him."

A week later Henry and Arch were on another foraging party; joined by two companies of the Second and four more of the Seventh Wisconsin. They traveled on a river transport a short distance and disembarked near a small town. As the men approached the town, Rebel cavalry appeared and, dismounting, began firing. It was apparent the enemy had not scouted the Union infantry well; as the front company deployed as skirmishers and the others moved into line of battle behind them, the true size of the force was seen. The southern horsemen, in a panic, quickly tried to remount to escape. One volley from the western men was sufficient to empty all but a few of the saddles. As the survivors rode away, the two companies of the Second were ordered to fall out and tend to the wounded up ahead. As Arch and Henry were turning over one body, Henry recognized the man as Luke, the soldier he had spoken with so long ago after the battle at Antietam. He found it hard to believe it had only been six months. It saddened him that another person he had met was gone; the war was harder to face when it became personal.

The detachment completed their foraging and returned to camp the next day with 12 wagons of food and 14 horses they had liberated from the Confederate cavalry. This was the last time Henry and Company H went on one of the expeditions until spring came. Their time in camp over the next month was a return to the usual routine of drill, standing guard, inspections and the normal boredom. Only once did Henry see Captain Patterson, when General Wadsworth and his staff rode by the Iron Brigade camp to the cheers of the men. The Captain had honored his promise though; the next day two boxes of bacon, more than 20 pounds, were delivered to Henry with compliments. After they ate their fill, Henry and Arch were the most popular two men in the regiment for a day.

Chapter 21

April 1863

General Hooker was the new commanding officer of the Army of the Potomac. He had taken over from General Burnside back in January and had done much to improve the morale of the Army. Food, both variety and availability, had been a major problem and the men were growing weary of a diet of salt pork, hardtack and coffee. General Hooker improved the way food was purchased and transported to the troops. Men like Captain Patterson, who knew how to run a business, were brought in to oversee the Quartermaster Corps and improve the supply situation. Vegetables and fruits began to arrive, both canned and freeze-dried, called desiccated; these were easily added to meat for soups or stews and helped prevent sickness like scurvy; the men enjoyed the wider variety of tastes.

A sure sign of spring in the camp was the increased attention to appearance, both of the men and their uniforms. The scent of soap drifted through the camp as they washed themselves and scrubbed dirty laundry. Leather was blackened and polished, metal was cleaned and shined; reviews were held to show off the army to dignitaries. The first was held for General Hooker, accompanied by the other generals in the First Corps. A few days later, President Lincoln and his family arrived at the camp and another review was held. The men were again formed into ranks by Division, Brigade and

Regiment and marched past a reviewing stand where the President, his wife and a son, and various officers stood. After the entire First Corps had passed by, President Lincoln mounted a horse and rode through the assembled Corps. He stopped in front of the Iron Brigade, dismounted and strode to where Arch and Henry stood. Lincoln stepped in front of Arch and, smiling, said "Were you and I not the two rails split by a portly sergeant at Antietam? I am glad to know you are well and still with us in this fight." Arch was absolutely flabbergasted at this; he managed to stammer out "Why, th-th-thank you Mr President, sir". The men of the Brigade let out three husky "Hoorahs!!" for their nation's leader as Lincoln moved down the line to another unit. His visit and personal touch and words went far to instill a greater pride in his army, the Army of the Potomac.

As the weeks went by, new troops were arriving to bulk up the regiments and to replace some units that had enlisted for only two years at the start of the war. Everywhere Henry looked he saw a growing number of tents and more guns parked in the artillery camps. He knew it would soon be the time to begin another campaign, one more attempt to take Richmond and end the war. He also sensed a stronger determination among the veterans; they all seemed to know that the fighting this year would be even harder and deadlier than 1862. Both sides were smarter and had more deadly weapons than before; both had also begun to appreciate digging in for defense. They knew that honor wouldn't stop a bullet as well as a log wall or a pile of dirt.

Henry received another letter from his father just before the middle of the month. James was down the Mississippi River as part of General Grant's army that was attempting to capture Vicksburg. Apparently he was very busy as the camps down there were full of sicknesses like malaria and swamp fever. Henry and Arch together sat and wrote a letter back describing their camp and the feeling that a campaign would soon be underway. Neither of them could know that as they were writing the letter, General Hooker was finalizing plans for that very operation, one that would involve the entire Army of the Potomac, all 100,000 or more men.

Four days later, as Henry and a few others from Company H were on a detail getting some cattle from the army's main herd to bring back for butchering, they noticed several cavalry regiments beginning to head out to the north and northwest. It looked bigger than just another expedition; this one had power with it. Henry counted eight cannon in line with one of the columns. He mentioned it to Arch when he got back to camp. Arch puffed on his pipe and replied, "Well, I for one have thought we've been loafing around a bit too long. Lad, I think it's time we make sure we've got all we need and only what we need. We'll be leaving here in a day or two, for sure."

Chapter 22

Chancellorsville

"So we'll be crossing in the pontoon boats just before first light. The Rebs will be sleeping and their sentries will be most tired about then. Corporal McCollum, you'll be in charge of one of the pontoons; pick four of your strongest to paddle it, the rest of your men will lie down in the boats. There's no need to stand and make yourself a target until you get across the river. The Sixth Wisconsin and 24th Michigan will be giving covering fire from this side and our artillery will be ready to let loose as well if need be. Sixteen men to a boat; four paddlers and 12 in the bottom. Is that understood?" Lieutenant Humphrey was a good company officer. He had been with them since he signed up as a private back in May of 1861 and had risen through the ranks. He would be in the first boat to leave shore.

"Where are those damned boats?" Arch was cross when he got nervous, and that alone made Henry more restless. "It's almost sunup and they're still not here. It will be the devil to pay if we have to cross in daylight. I scouted their position yesterday and it's a strong set of entrenchments on top of the far bank. Just remember, boys, no one stands up and the paddlers go like hell." There was a quiet rolling, like thunder, behind them and, without looking Henry knew it was the wagons with the pontoons. They didn't have full darkness but it was better than bright sunlight.

The men moved as quietly as they could, unloaded their boat and headed down to the water. Four men each carried two muskets; their own and a paddler's. Four others carried their paddles and the final eight men hoisted the pontoon up and, four on each side, carried and slid it down the bank. Though it was still before the sun was up, the noise of dozens of pontoons coming down the bank was enough to wake up the Rebels across the water. As the western men got into the boats, they could hear the first pops of rifle fire from the top of the opposite bank. Instantly there was the sound of their own men firing back; then the cannon joined in and the next few minutes were full of that familiar smoke and noise and sweat and fear and screaming and blood and all that went into a fight. Henry was lying down in the pontoon when a paddler above him fell over with a grunt and a splash. He jumped up and managed to grab the paddle in the water, swinging it into a first stroke. He was glad he had handled boats on the river back home with Marcus; but this was not a swift canoe. He strained with the size and weight of what felt like an overloaded barge.

Henry looked to the left; in another pontoon he saw General Wadsworth himself, standing tall; his horse was swimming behind the boat. The General was smoking a cigar and seem almost nonchalant about the whole crossing. He reached up for his hat and, looking at it, stuck two fingers through a couple of fresh bullet holes. He put the hat back on and looked straight ahead. Henry was amazed and impressed; glad that there were leaders like Wadsworth. Now the boat thumped on the bottom and men jumped up and scrambled out, into the knee deep water and ran to shore. Some were already pulling themselves up the bank using tree roots and being shoved from behind by their mates. The Rebs couldn't shoot down on them without standing up themselves, making fine targets as they were silhouetted against the rising sun. In less than ten minutes it was all over. Blue coated men were advancing over the top of the embankment and Henry could just make out some men in gray trying to get away ahead of them; most would jump up and get a step or two then tumble down like rag dolls.

The man next to Henry, from the Seventh Wisconsin, jumped up and yelled; the noise was enough to make a person cringe. Arch turned to Henry and said, "It's one of the Ojibway boys, there's a bunch in the Seventh." The man's screams and shrieks were joined by the shouts and hurrahs of a hundred voices now. They had made it across the river, but at what cost no one yet knew. Henry looked back down to the river and saw men already retrieving a few bodies out of the water, even as the engineers were laying the first pontoons of a new bridge. In an hour there would be wagons and cannon and such coming across; the new campaign was underway.

Henry woke to the sound of distant thunder; not the kind that accompanies rain. This noise comes with death and destruction. It meant that General Hooker, with the majority of the Army had found and engaged General Lee's Army of Northern Virginia. Now he knew that the job they had performed yesterday in crossing the river had been a feint, a diversion to draw some of the Confederates away from the main attack. Once again Arch was already up and the coffee was boiling over the fire. "Good mornin' lad; a cup of rio will open your eyes and start your day." Arch handed Henry a steaming tin mug of the brew and a cracker. Henry thanked his uncle and mumbled, "I wonder what today will bring?"

Chapter 23

May 1863

Missouri

"Colonel, I'm not sure I understand what this means; I only arrived here two days ago and now I'm to travel to Washington City?" James McCollum, wearing a uniform with the rank of Captain in the Medical Corps, was standing in an office at Jefferson Barracks. He had been ordered to report to St Louis and had no idea why.

"Captain, the Army giveth and the Army taketh away. Apparently you are known by someone out east, perhaps the work you've done in Wisconsin is of a type they seem to need. I'm not part of this decision, just the messenger. Get your things together, there's a steamboat leaving in the morning that will take you up the Ohio River and you can board a train to Washington from there. I've been informed that the 23rd has an assistant surgeon and will get along for the time being."

James saluted and left the office, bewildered at who would have thought to change his orders. This army life would take some getting used to he supposed. When he got back to his room, he quickly packed and sat down to write a couple of letters.

Chapter 24

May 1863

Virginia

The sound of the fighting off to the northwest had been quieting down through the day. Rumors had been drifting through the camp that, finally, a battle seemed to be going well for the Union. Men began to talk of being home in time for summer. Arch shook his head at each report; he had heard all of this too many times to give it any real value. Henry seemed to not pay it any attention at all. Since his return from Wisconsin, he had gradually begun to withdraw into himself; Arch wasn't quite sure what to make of it. He just seemed a littler quieter and sad.

The Rebs in their front hadn't tried to push them back across the river. They seemed content to let the Yanks stay there and, except for a few shots by skirmishers, everything here was quiet. Later that evening, as the men were gathered in small groups around fires eating what food they had, the battle sounds in the distance suddenly grew into a crescendo of noise. It was too far away to discern who was getting the upper hand in it; though a short time later as the sun was finally setting, officers could be seen scurrying around. It was a sign that they were about to move out again, but where to was anyone's guess.

Henry and Arch could not know that another defeat was in the making for the Army of the Potomac. General Lee and "Stonewall" Jackson had done it again; Jackson had marched his corps around the flank of the Union position and launched an attack that struck like a hammer, rolling up the right of the Federal line and causing another panic. General Reynold's First Corp, including the Iron Brigade, was ordered to recross the river and march to the aid of Hooker's army. It was becoming all too familiar and the men grumbled through their night march.

By morning they had reached one of the pontoon bridges that lead to the rear of their army. They could see some of the effects of Lee's attack; there were large groups of wounded, in and out of ambulances being moved to the safer areas on the east side of the river. Along with the injured were hundreds of others, men too afraid to fight were heading to the rear; most had thrown away their weapons and equipment in their haste to keep ahead of Jackson's Rebels.

The sight of the First Corps, with the Iron Brigade in the lead, moving toward the sounds of battle caused many of those retreating to stop and cheer. The western men seemed to straighten up and quicken their pace at the sound. Arch turned to Henry and said, "Looks like we have to rescue the easterners once again. Wouldn't it be grand if they could find someone else to pull their feet out of the fire just once?" Henry grinned, pulled his hat a bit tighter on his head and replied, "Well, uncle; I've been thinking on this march. It seems to me that the only way I'm ever going to get home to stay is to pitch in a bit harder than I have in the past. If we don't, this war will never end. It will just go on and on. I'll be eighteen in two weeks and I've already been in this fight for nearly two years. From now until it's over, I'll be right in the thick of it every chance I get. It either ends sooner for all of us, or it'll be over quicker for me."

Chapter 25

May 1863

Wisconsin

"I'm serious, Catherine, I cannot stay put here one more day when I read about all the men dying and wounded; the three men closest to me are all in this war and I will not stand by and pass my days fretting about them any longer. This morning's paper is full of stories about this terrible fight at Chancellorsville and General Grant's campaign against Vicksburg. Surely there is somewhere I can help as a nurse; James has used me to assist him for years. My skills will be an asset to the army just like his. I just don't know which way to go, with Henry and Arch in the east and James down in Arkansas."

"Sister, what would your husband think of you just showing up at his camp? You know there is no place for a woman in the field with the soldiers; at least, not unless you're a laundress, or..." The knock at the door stopped Catherine in mid sentence. She went to answer and found a neighbor outside. She had been in town doing some shopping and had stopped at the post office to send her own son a package. There was a letter for Marie and she had brought it back with her. Marie said it was from James and began to read it.

"That settles my only question. For some reason, he doesn't know exactly why, James has been ordered to

Washington City. He thinks it may be the new hospitals being built there; doctors with experience in certain injuries are being gathered together. I'll have to arrange transportation for myself; I suppose I could leave as soon as the day after tomorrow." With a peaceful resolve, Marie began her journey with a step toward her room. By the end of that day she had arranged her transportation to the east, sent a telegram followed by a letter of instructions back to Dekorra concerning their home, purchased a few things she would need on the trip and had written to Henry and Arch, outlining what she was doing.

The following day Marie spent packing what she would need into two trunks and had the remainder shipped back to Dekorra. She arranged for the two trunks to be brought to the train station in Kenosha. Her travels would take her to Chicago and on to Washington City by way of Philadelphia and Baltimore.

Chapter 26

Virginia

The past few days had been full of confusion and marching; the marching punctuated with numerous periods of waiting, both in formation on the roads and lying on the ground while officers tried to determine where they were to go next. The brigade had spent the first night in line on the right of the whole Federal army. The next morning when General Hooker ordered a retreat back across the river; the Iron Brigade was, again, assigned as the rear guard for the retreat. Then had come the days of confusion until the westerners were finally ordered back to where they had started the campaign down across from Fredericksburg. They had spent a week wearing out their brogans and hadn't fired a weapon. Their spirits were pretty low.

General Reynolds ordered a few more small excursions into the territory to their south in order to forage and to assist cavalry patrols that were out scouting the Rebels. Henry and Arch went on one such march and saw the beauty of a part of the country that had not been scarred by the war. When they returned a few days later the regiment received their first mail in nearly a month; in it were letters from both of Henry's parents.

"I don't read here that Father knows Mother is also on her way to Washington. Imagine his expression when she shows up there as well. I'll bet there will be hell to pay!!" Henry was able to even laugh a bit with the thought of how his father's face would look when they met up. For this Arch was glad; he had been very worried about his nephew on the last march. Henry had volunteered time and again to go out ahead of the regiment, taking chances that would have proved very dangerous if any shooting had started. Arch was convinced now that Henry was looking for trouble either because he truly felt indestructible or as a way out; if he were dead he wouldn't go through life with a terribly scarred face.

Now they were in camp again and quickly settled into that familiar routine of drill, standing guard, and filling too many hours with whatever they could find. Henry couldn't even write home now because "home" was somewhere on the move approaching Washington. Arch tried to get him to read some books on history and mathematics, to improve his mind for after the war. Henry would give him the same blank stare each time, as if to say "What for?" Henry no longer spoke about life after the fighting stopped. He wouldn't look in a mirror either, not that he had to, because he didn't shave and practically no one combed hair. Only when the troops were inspected by General Reynolds did they have to work hard at looking military; and again when the Governor of Michigan visited to present the 24th with their own black hats. The regiment had earned them at Fredericksburg six months earlier, but now was a more convenient time for the politicians to make something of the event. Finally the entire brigade wore the tall, regulation black Hardee with the ostrich feathers blowing in the wind.

A few days later, in the early part of June, Henry and Arch were on picket duty along the river and watched as the Rebels held a review on the battlefield of the past December. It seemed like all of General Lee's

Confederates were there, except Stonewall Jackson who had been killed in the fighting at Chancellorsville a month ago. Arch knew this was a sure sign that the Rebels would be moving soon; it was the army way.

The next day they heard around the supper fire that the enemy was, indeed, gone. Now the game was afoot. The Union cavalry would be out looking for them while General Stuart's own horsemen would try to keep Lee and his army hidden, screening them with quick strikes here and there. Eventually someone would report Rebel infantry on the move and the chase would begin. There was always the hope that this time when the two armies met, the advantage would be with the north.

Chapter 27

June 1863

"What do you mean, she's in Washington? What in heaven's name would make her strike out on her own like that?" James was not nearly as angry as he was bewildered; he had just been told of Marie's journey to find him out east. Her sister, Catherine, had picked him up at the station after he wired from Chicago that he was stopping by for a week or so on his own way to the nation's capital. Now he ordered a ticket for the next train back to Chicago so he could also head east to try to find her. The train would leave the next morning, so he spent the night at his sister-in-law's house while she tried to explain all that had happened while he had been to St Louis and back.

"James, you know Marie has always been the strongest in our family; I believe it's what attracted you to her in the beginning. Actually, I believe Marie will be more in her element in Washington than here in Wisconsin. Don't forget, she was raised by my father to be a leader, even it it's frowned upon by our society today. Both of us believe it's a matter of time before women will be much more than wives, though that is a noble role." James knew better than to be drawn into this unwinnable discussion; he had once been on the receiving end of both Catherine and Marie's "the future of womanhood" talk. He knew the qualities of his wife and other women.

"You know, Catherine, there is a new doctor, a woman in fact, highly respected by some of her colleagues, even me. Her name is Mary Walker and is serving in the army right now. I'm not angry with Marie, I applaud her convictions. She might have discussed it with me, that's all."

"Really, James; how long would that conversation have taken by mail, or even by telegraph? She felt a need to go; she told me you had the same feeling just a short time ago. If I know my sister, she is at this moment, arranging a position for herself just where she can do the most good, as expertly as a man would."

"I'll have to be careful that I don't end up taking orders from her, I suppose." James said this with a chuckle and a twinkle in his eye. Catherine looked at him with a solemn and serious expression.

"Don't be too sure you won't be following her directions soon."

In fact, Marie had just completed an interview with the director of nursing at one of the hospitals outside the city, in Maryland. Her duties, as soon as she procured the necessary clothing, would be to supervise the care of wounded soldiers...hundreds of them. There was a critical shortage of women nurses who had actually worked in the medical field. Her experiences as the wife of a doctor in the Midwest would prove invaluable to the hospital. While she had intended to begin as a volunteer, she discovered she was to be paid for her services, and this was something she had never experienced.

Marie was staying at the Willard Hotel in Washington; it was known as the "center of the capital society scene", notably by the writer Nathaniel Hawthorne. In the few days since her arrival, she had already met several congressmen and a senator. Marie had even viewed President Lincoln on one of his carriage rides, escorted by a squad of cavalrymen. The entire city had a military feel, with uniforms nearly outnumbering the civilian clothing. In her own way, Marie wondered why with so many officers, the war had not already been won.

Two days later Marie was situated in her new surroundings; several whitewashed buildings that still smelled of newly cut pine. Four of the long hospital barracks surrounded five or six smaller buildings that housed the bakery, kitchen, laundry, offices and sleeping quarters for the doctors on duty. Inside each barrack were rows of beds, each with mattress and clean sheets; one of the nurses gave her a quick tour of the facility and explained that patients would begin to arrive this very evening. The first were being moved from the patent office, where they had been housed among the display cases and filing cabinets of that building. Even churches and the treasury building had wounded soldiers in them. This hospital was one of twelve; some were already finished with others still to be built. It was understood that the Sanitary Commission had played a big part in the design of the hospital and the Christian Commission would also be on hand to assist the wounded in writing letters, reading to them, and helping them recover from the trauma of war.

In Virginia, the Army of the Potomac was on the move. This time there were none of the usual “start and stop” aspects to it. The regiments, brigades, divisions and even whole corps were stepping out with purpose. The days were hot and dry; the dust was as deep as a man’s shoe tops, raising huge clouds that the men struggled to keep pace in. Miles upon miles, twenty seven the first day, passed by as men dropped out of ranks on the side of the road. Some actually died in mid-step, overcome by the heat and the dust. When they stopped at night, no camps were set up; the men dropped where they stood and fell asleep for as long as their officers would allow. The Rebels had stolen a march on them and there was desperate work to catch up.

The Iron Brigade was passing through familiar country now; they were just a few miles from Brawner Farm. It was here they had met the Stonewall Brigade and gone toe to toe with them until night fell back in '62. It was not quite a year ago and it seemed like an eternity to some. They fell out for a few hours sleep on the same spot they had camped the night of that struggle. Henry, even in his own exhaustion, couldn't stop thinking that this was where he first had heard that Marcus was missing. The year before that, they had camped near here the night before First Bull Run. To him it was a lifetime ago; a whole face was his the first time he slept here. No monster to girls then; he had sent the tintype home to his folks, a likeness of a young man out to conquer the world. Now he felt all used up; there was little more inside him to give.

They slept for three hours and were on the road again before the sun rose. It was better in the dark; you couldn't see the dust and it was much cooler. The road ahead was lit by torches alongside; sometimes whole trees were burned so the men could see where to march. Word was passed down the line that the Rebels were in Maryland, next to the Pennsylvania border. Rumors were, they were heading for Philadelphia or even Washington. There were no Federal troops up that way; only state militia and they wouldn't stand up to the battle hardened southerners with their Rebel yell. More rumors circulated that General Hooker had been replaced; General-in-Chief Halleck in Washington had relieved him and appointed General George Meade to command the Army of the Potomac. Meade was a Pennsylvania man and would certainly fight his army hard against a southern invasion of his home state.

The men crossed into Maryland at Edwards Ferry, just like before Antietam. It was almost spooky how it reminded all of them of last year. That night they camped at Turner's Gap, right on the field where they had earned the name Iron Brigade just nine months earlier. They could see headboards above the graves of their mates that had fallen that night; the men they, themselves, had buried. Some of the writing on the boards was already faded. Sad to think that no one would remember you once your name had washed off your grave marker. They marched the next day through Monocacy and on to Emmittsburg.

"The word from Baltimore is that the Rebs are in Chambersburg and some of Stuart's cavalry is heading for Philadelphia." The man was a new replacement in the company, had been with them since just after Fredericksburg. He had not seen any real fighting but considered himself a veteran; Arch would admit he'd learned how to march at least. They were conversing around a rare fire, the first they had been allowed in three days. They were given time to rest, eat some hot food, and bathe. It was the first washing some had enjoyed in weeks. After the refreshing river dip, all of them were settled down before they slept.

"Well, now, if they're all those places, we ought to be able to pick them apart in detail. Trouble would be more real if they have time to concentrate. This army is spread from here down to Centerville, nearly 50 miles. Word is, Lee has over 100,000 men and we've only got First and Eleventh Corps nearby, maybe 14,000. Doesn't sound very promising to me." This bit of wisdom came from a newly appointed officer from another company who had come over to light his pipe. Henry and Arch looked at each other, shrugged and drank some more coffee.

In a moment Arch spoke up. "The way I figure, if they're moving so much faster than we are, how come we don't see any of them lying by the road? If they'd had 100,000 at Chancellorsville, we'd be speaking southron by now. I think we ought to just hunker down inside ourselves and find that spark we're gonna need in a few more days when the words are done and the bullets are flyin'." Henry appreciated his uncle and his sense of what to say when he spoke. He, himself, was almost looking forward to a fight. He had to prove he was still worthy of living. The past couple of months he'd been thinking all he deserved was to die; not that he really wished for it. He wanted one more chance to do good, to beat some Rebs so bad that he beat the fight right out of them. It seemed to him like defending his country was a good way of doing it; maybe that's why the Rebs fought so damned hard in Virginia.

Henry woke the next morning to the sound of cavalry trotting by. It was the brigade of General Buford; as they went by the infantry, good natured greetings and challenges were exchanged. "You boys better hurry, hate to have you miss a party" and "Mebbe you'ns ought to stay put, might be a tad unhealthful up ahead". The westerners knew and respected this group of cavalrymen; it was Buford's boys that had gone ahead of them just before the Brawner Farm fight. This was yet another reminder of those days and what might lay up the road in Pennsylvania.

Today the pace of the march slowed a bit. The men guessed it was so the rest of the army could catch up; Arch thought it was because no one knew for sure just what General Lee was up to. No one knew that, in fact, General Lee was groping around blind himself. He had allowed Stuart and his cavalry to ride off, too far to stay in contact with the main army. Now Lee had no way of scouting the location of the Yankees; both sides slowly edged toward each other. It was strange; the Rebels were coming from the north and the Yanks from the south. Between them lay a town with seven roads leading into it; the place was called Gettysburg.

Chapter 28

June 1863

Washington City

"Good morning, Captain. I trust your journey was a safe and comfortable one. Did you happen to see any Rebels on your way through Pennsylvania? We've heard they are all over the southern part of that state. So close to here, it makes me a bit jumpy." The Major stood behind the counter, his arms barely able to reach beyond his substantial girth to pick up James' papers. "Let me see, Wisconsin to Mississippi and then back to here. You have been around lately, eh? Hmmmm, you're to be stationed at the new hospital just outside the city near Georgetown. You're fortunate that it's located inside the ring of new forts built to protect the city. If Lee and his horde come this way, they'd probably burn everything near here, like the British back in 1812."

"Excuse me Major, is it possible to delay my reporting to the hospital for one more day? My wife is in the city and I need to locate her. Can you recommend a hotel or other available rooms?"

"Certainly, you can find the Willard Hotel just a few blocks away. I'll have an orderly take your bags there if you'd like. I would imagine your wife herself is probably registered there; it's the finest in Washington City. You have until day after tomorrow to report to the hospital; I'm sure the Willard can arrange transport for you there." The major turned, moved a few feet to a large chair and sat, the chair creaking in protest.

James left the building and walked the eight blocks to the Willard. Lost in thought, his head down, he mumbled thanks to the doorman at the hotel and entered the lobby, nearly knocking down a woman leaving. "A thousand pardons, Ma'am. I wasn't looking....oh my Lord, Marie!!" He nearly crushed her in his embrace.

"Honestly, James. What are the chances of this? I came back here to leave a message for you where to find me. I'm overseeing the nurses at a new hospital near Georgetown. We can talk of that later; you look worn out and hungry. Let's do have a cold dinner and talk. Have you heard from Henry or your brother?"

Over a wonderful meal of cold chicken, fresh fruit and wine the two held hands and talked of the past months. James related his travels and frustration of having been in the army since January and having spent most of that time traveling. Marie was giddy with excitement about her new position at the hospital and the wonder that they would both be working there. She told him that the facility was already full, the battle of Chancellorsville had seen to that. "We've got nearly 1,500 beds full and could easily have that many more. It's a terrible thing to see them arrive; dirty, awful wounds. Some came in with bandages they had put on themselves. But a day or so later and they're bathed, fed good food and in a clean bed. It's a miracle how much that alone helps, lifts their spirits. The men themselves say that they try to avoid the field hospitals because of what they see there. The nurses are trying, along with the Sanitary Commission, to get permission to serve closer to the battle areas and try to work the same miracle there."

James added, "I am excited to see it in action. Trying to make a difference and improve things is exactly what drove me into this army. Listening to Henry and his story of what medical treatment he received; well, it convinced me that I needed to "pitch in" as well. Do you suppose we can get word of the Iron Brigade and where they are? With this invasion by the Confederates, I'm sure Henry and Arch are on their way to Pennsylvania, if they're not there already. The papers are calling it another Antietam, or at least it will be when the two armies collide. How do you suppose the hospitals will handle another 20,000 wounded?"

"James, please don't talk about this anymore. My heart is breaking at the thought of another battle like that. General Grant's siege at Vicksburg has already cost the north thousands dead and wounded. We don't even know how many have been killed in the city itself. This war is horrible and the killing is getting worse; it has to stop soon. Perhaps the two sides can reason together... I suppose that's not possible. As long as Jefferson Davis insists on slavery and an independent Confederacy, there's little hope of coming together. We must win the next battle and end this war if it means building a hundred more hospitals."

Chapter 29

Gettysburg

An officer on horseback rode up; he was one of General Reynold's aides. After speaking with Colonel Merideth, the Iron Brigade's commanding officer, the aide galloped off down the line to the next brigade. Meredith issued orders to the officers standing near him and then rode himself to alert the other regiments. Arch, Henry and several others sitting near them jumped up and began to gather their gear. Soon the sound of the long roll was heard and the men of the Second Wisconsin began to fall in to ranks on the road. Dimly in the distance could be heard a sound like far off thunder. Arch turned to Henry and said "Again, lad, into the storm. It looks like Buford's gone and found Bobby Lee."

The march up the Emmittsburg Road was a quieter one than in the days before. Each man was now certain that fighting would be at the end of this one. The Iron Brigade stepped out, led by the Sixth Wisconsin with the other regiments in line behind. They marched with a purpose, wearing expressions which showed that each was deep in personal thoughts, every one of them measuring their own fortitude; not one of them would willingly "*show the white feather*" by running away when the bullets started flying.

With each mile they covered, the sounds of battle ahead grew louder. They knew the dismounted cavalry was not able to hold back Rebel infantry forever; soon they could hear the deeper booms of the field artillery as it was brought up to support the southern attack. Buford's own artillery was answering, the flatter crack of the 3" ordnance rifles answering the Confederate 12 pounders. Soon the brigade was marching north, up the road between two ridges. They could just make out the *cupola* on a tall building ahead. The officers leading the march left the road, heading west through open fields and up the western ridge. Men were rushed out front to rip down fences that would slow the march while the smoke of the battle in front could be seen rising above the tree line. The men were ordered to the double quick, a sort of jogging run; it made it more difficult to load their muskets on the go.

As they reached the top of the ridge, they saw the back of the Union cavalry line; a long thin blue stretching to the north with the artillery in a road. The cupola they had spotted earlier was on a large building, a Lutheran seminary; there were Union signalmen in it wig-wagging their signal flags. Now the order was given to move into battle line behind the cavalry. Further in front could be seen the thick lines of Confederate infantry, with more columns up the road coming from the west. The Second Wisconsin was ordered to slide to the right and then move forward against a Rebel thrust just breaking the Union cavalry line. The regiment advanced, Henry and Arch in the second line, and received a volley from the enemy. Dozens of westerners went down under the hail of lead. With a shout the Second stood tall and delivered their own fire; then they lowered their rifles and charged with the bayonet against four times their number. The entire Confederate brigade ahead of them stopped, turned and began to run. They had cleared the forward slope of the ridge and captured nearly 75 of the enemy, including General Archer, a brigade commander. There was no time to celebrate.

Colonel Merideth ordered the regiment to stand fast while the rest of the brigade came up. There had been bitter fighting to their left and the other regiments needed a bit more time to drive the Rebs back. All together they advanced toward some woods in front. Rebel skirmishers were in there and had to be removed. Lee had not wanted a general engagement here and it took some time for the southerners to form their other brigades into battle lines. The Iron Brigade prepared to receive their attack in the woods, knowing it had to hold, along with the rest of First Corps, until the Eleventh and Twelfth Corps could arrive behind them.

Henry looked to his right and saw Captain Patterson. The Captain was pointing to the front as he was shouting to be heard. When he approached, Patterson said he needed skirmishers to go forward as the brigade prepared to move back to regroup; they would cover the backward movement. Henry volunteered before Arch could say a word. The boy was up on his feet and, crouching low, moved up behind a tree. The word to fall back was given and the rest of the regiment slowly stepped back, keeping their guns pointed to the enemy. They moved out of the woods, back across a field and up behind a rail fence at the top of the slope. All the while, bullets were kicking up dust and snipping leaves and branches off the trees and bushes. As the Confederates began their next assault, it was time for the skirmishers to fall back. They did it on the run. Henry had never run so hard, not pausing to turn and fire. There was no way he would be able to reload running this fast. He could see Arch now, waving him on, motioning for Henry to join the line next to him. As he bounded over the fence and turned, he could see hundreds of the Rebels pouring out of the woods. He had heard them screaming their yell as he had left the woods. Now he picked out an officer and raised his Springfield to his shoulder, exhaling to steady his aim. As he fired he felt something slam into his side, just below the ribs.

Henry fell back, his rifle slipping from his grip. He tried to sit up and couldn't; Arch was leaning over him in an instant. "Lie still, lad. Another and I are goin' to move you back. You're not goin' to like this a bit. Hold on." As Arch and a mate started to move him, it felt like someone was tearing him in half. Henry could not stop the scream that rushed out of his chest and passed his lips. "Oh, God...oh, God..." He fought for breath and felt like someone was holding him under water. Arch had dragged him back about 20 yards behind a small shed. There were other men there as well; one next to Henry was missing an arm above the elbow, his life and blood were flowing out of the stump onto the ground. The man seemed to turn a bluish white even as Henry watched.

Arch found another man to help, the first had been cut down as they were dragging Henry. The two carried Henry back to a barn; inside were nearly a hundred soldiers of both sides. A couple of Rebels were helping a Union hospital steward tend to the crowd. "Set him there...ohhhh, through both sides. Sorry, Corporal, there's nothing that can be done with him." The steward moved off to check on another being brought in. Arch gently laid Henry on some straw and knelt next to him.

"Henry, lad, can you hear me? It's Uncle Arch, boy, can you hear me?" The tears were welling up in Arch's eyes as he spoke.

"Yes, uncle.....it's alright. I knew this was going to happen one day. When you see Mother and Father.... tell them I was brave. Thank you for being with me."

Arch stayed with Henry until he stopped breathing and his face relaxed. "The face of an angel" Arch thought as he folded Henry's arms on his chest. He took a piece of paper and wrote "Henry McCollum, Second Wisconsin, Iron Brigade" on it, pinning it to Henry's sack coat. "You'll not be buried in an unmarked grave, lad. Not like Marcus. I'll always know where you are. I promise."

Chapter 30

Washington City

"Doctor McCollum? Excuse me, sir; I have orders here for you and the rest of the hospital staff. You're to pack and be ready to move by tomorrow morning, sir. The entire staff will be on a train for Pennsylvania; you are to set up a new hospital at Gettysburg, sir. A detail is already there putting up the tents and the necessary supplies should be there when you arrive." The Lieutenant saluted, handed James the papers and left.

James had felt this would happen. Something was drawing him to that place ever since he'd read of the fighting a week earlier. The papers had announced the victory; Lee had been whipped and was heading back south. Meade was slowly following him; this did not please the President who wanted him to move the army faster and catch the Confederates. There was mention of the Iron Brigade but the full lists of dead and wounded had not been printed; what was mentioned were the more than 50,000 casualties suffered by both sides. Things were very bad in the town of 2,500; wells were dry and water was being brought in by wagons. Every house in Gettysburg was a hospital and it had taken a full week to bury all the dead; the 10,000 dead horses had been piled up and burned.

At first, the nation celebrated on the Fourth of July. The battle had been won on the third; the next day Vicksburg surrendered to General Grant. The telegraph brought that news within hours of the event and people were amazed at the speed news traveled now. Then the horrible facts began to appear. The battle in Pennsylvania eclipsed Antietam and Shiloh combined.

James walked to the building where Marie worked. He told her the orders and she immediately began the process for the nurses to relocate. Staff from the hospital next to this one would be doing double duty for awhile, at least until new help could be obtained.

Chapter 31

August 1863

Marie was hard at work. This hospital used tents, piles of straw on the ground in lieu of beds, had no bakery and water was as precious as gold. They also had more wounded than would have fit in the Georgetown facility. Still, she was near James and they could spend what little time away from the job together. It troubled her greatly that there had been no word from Arch or Henry since the battle, more than six weeks ago. Marie looked out of the tent opening and saw a tall, lanky fellow walking away. As he moved, she recognized his gait. "Arch, Archibald McCollum, is that you?", she cried.

Arch turned around and hurried to her. "Hello, sister. I've been lookin' for you all day. A man could get lost easily in this tent city. I don't know where James is at present."

"Oh, he's in the surgical tent. You can't see him for a few more hours, I'm sure. What are you doing here....and where's Henry?" Even as she asked, she could see the pain in Arch's eyes. "No...dear God, no..." she cried as he reached for her.

They were able to arrange to see James right away. As the three sat shedding tears together, Arch managed to tell them of the first day at Gettysburg and what had happened. "It's no news a letter can carry, I'm afraid. It took some time to find you; I had to write Dekorra and Kenosha and wait for an answer. Then a walk to Washington City from Virginia and now a train here. I still have two more days until I have to head back to the regiment. My captain was kind to let me go to find you; he said it's the least he could do for the man that delivered him two strapping boys."

Epilogue

November 1863

Gettysburg

The town was packed with visitors. The orator, Edward Everett of Massachusetts, was to deliver the dedication of the new cemetery this afternoon. Some said that President Lincoln had even been invited to attend. People paid to sleep on porches; there were no rooms available at any price.

James and Marie were still working at the hospital, though the number of wounded was down below 3,000 now. Arch was one of them; he had been hit in the left arm in Virginia and James had managed to get him assigned to the hospital here for recuperation. Now they were standing on a street as the dedication parade passed by, the coaches with dignitaries and the President, then the army band and a few regiments of Pennsylvania militia. As it ended, people began to make their way to the new cemetery for a good spot to hear Everett's oration.

As they made their way over to hear the speech, a carriage stopped next to them. James and Marie were astonished to see President Lincoln sitting in it. The President leaned down, tipped his hat to Marie and said to Arch, "Now here is a member of the famed Iron Brigade I look up to.... it is good to see you again,

Corporal, and I sincerely hope your wound is not troubling."

"Thank you Mr President, it's fine, sir. Be healed and with the black hatter's before long."

The President smiled and his carriage moved on. Arch turned to James and said, "You know, that's the third time I've had the chance to speak with that man. Now, what do you say we avoid Mr Everett's talk; I've heard he's a bit long winded. I'd like to see where Henry is, I've a promise to keep."

The three walked through the cemetery and found the Wisconsin section. Standing in front of grave #B-13, Arch removed his hat, bowed his head and said quietly, "You see, lad, I'll always know where you are."

GLOSSARY

TERM	DEFINITION
Abolitionists	People, mostly up north, who were against slavery.
Brigade	Normally three to five regiments, about 4,000 men.
Brogans	Shoes worn by civil war soldiers; they were neither right nor left.
Cannister	A metal can of iron balls; like a giant shotgun shell.
Capping	Putting a percussion cap on the rifle so it would fire.
Company	Normally a group of 100 men.
Confederate	The southern states in the war; the Confederate States.
Corps	Normally two or more divisions, about 14,000 men.
Cupola	A walkway around the top of a tower or tall building.
Division	Normally two or more brigades, about 8,000 men.
Drill	Practice as marching in formation; fighting as a unit.

Free Soiler	Those who believed new lands being settled should not be opened for slavery.
Long Roll	A drum beat calling the men to formation.
Militia	Civilians who were paid by a state to train and serve like soldiers, like today's National Guard.
Minie ball	Civil War bullets.
Mustered	To be signed up in the Regular Army as a soldier.
On Their Arms	To sleep holding your rifle on the open ground.
Picket	Standing guard away from the camp.
Reb	Slang for Rebel or Confederate; a southern soldier.
Rebel yell	A high pitched noise rebels made when they charged; similar to a coyote.
Regiment	Normally ten companies of infantry; about 1,000 men.
Route Step	To march at your own pace, not in perfect step.
Seccesh	Southern troops; also rebs or confederates.

See the Elephant	Slang for the first time you were in combat.
Show the White Feather	To run away from a battle; to be a coward.
Skedaddle	Slang for an unorganized mob on a retreat.
Skirmisher	Soldiers spread out in front of an advancing regiment.
Sutler	Merchants who sold items to the soldiers.
Tintype	Early photographs were printed on metal, not paper.
Union	The northern states in the war; the United States.
Zouave	Troops dressed in colorful uniforms patterned after North African armies.

Other Books by Michael Eckers

Northern Colors

The Boys of Wasioja

Copies of this book,

"Wisconsin Iron"

may be obtained by contacting the author directly at:

michael.eckers@gmail.com

Contact the author to discuss volume discounts for schools or fundraising opportunities for non-profit organizations such as local historical society projects or American Civil War programs.

Michael Eckers has presented historical talks covering the American Civil War and the Dakota Conflict of 1862 publicly for more than a decade.

If you are part of a group interested in hearing his presentation, feel free to contact him at the above e-mail address.

Second Wisconsin Monument at Gettysburg

(Author's collection)